# CLIFFHANGERS

## HOLD ON TIGHT!

### The most exciting books you've ever read!

**by**
**Eric Weiner**

## RUNAWAY BUS!

Freddy is always late for school. But today, it's not his fault—he's chasing bank robbers in a school bus with no brakes!

## DON'T LOOK DOWN!

Taking care of her neighbor's cat is a real easy job for Denise. But she didn't know she'd have to walk out on a thirteenth-floor ledge to do it!

## THRILL RIDE!

Only one thing scares Annie more than riding the huge roller coaster, the Serpent . . . getting stuck upside down on the biggest loop!

## Collect them all...
## IF YOU DARE!

### AND DON'T EVEN
### *TRY* TO PUT THEM DOWN!

**CLIFFHANGERS**

*Thrill Ride!*

# ERIC WEINER

BERKLEY BOOKS, NEW YORK

THRILL RIDE!

A Berkley Book / published by arrangement with
the author

PRINTING HISTORY
Berkley edition / September 1996

The Putnam Berkley World Wide Web site address is
http://www.berkley.com

ISBN: 0-425-14985-4

BERKLEY®
Berkley Books are published by The Berkley Publishing Group,
200 Madison Avenue, New York, New York 10016.
BERKLEY and the "B" design
are trademarks belonging to Berkley Publishing Corporation.

PRINTED IN THE UNITED STATES OF AMERICA

10  9  8  7  6  5  4  3

# CHAPTER 1

**W**HAT WAS THAT?

I sit up in bed, straining my ears.

It's almost midnight. Dad's away on a business trip. Mom's asleep. So's our dog, Truman. He's lying under the piano downstairs, snoring loudly. But from my older brother's room down the hall I hear these—

Tiny sounds.

Little creaks of drawers and teeny rattles of hangers.

Sounds like Stu is getting dressed. In the middle of the night.

Which can only mean one thing . . .

He's up to something.

But what?

Whatever it is, he's going to leave me out.

I'm only twelve. Worse, I'm a girl. Stuart's fifteen. And his goal in life is to leave his younger sister out of whatever he does. It could be anything. Like if Mom asks him to bike down to the store and get some toilet paper, I'll say, "Hey, Stu, I'll come with ya." And he'll say, "No tagging."

You would think he'd like the company.

Stuart is this total math-whiz science genius, plus he's got pretty bad pimples sprinkled over his forehead and cheeks. He's geeky thin, shy, quiet, and he reads a lot. What I'm trying to say is, Stuart doesn't have a ton of friends that I can see.

Neither do I. Which is why I'm always trying to hang out with him. But he almost always says no. Or if he lets me come, he'll charge a favor, like I have to wash the dishes when it's his turn.

Wow. The floor feels like ice on my bare feet as I tiptoe into the hall. I stand stock-still, listening hard.

It's November. The wind is so strong it rattles the windows. Downstairs our dog stops snoring and makes these sounds like he's swallowing something. The little cutie . . . Truman must be dreaming about food.

But—

I don't hear a thing from Stu's room.

So . . . maybe I was wrong. Maybe my ears were playing tricks on me and Stu's asleep, like *I* should be.

Maybe.

Only one way to find out.

As I inch down the hall I try to avoid the floorboards that make loud creaks when you step on them. Stu's door is ajar. I stand outside, listening. Still don't hear anything—except my own breathing.

He's tricking me. I know it.

Annie, you're getting paranoid. What would Stu be doing in the middle of the night?

Something fun, that's what. Something dangerous, grown-up, cool. Just the kind of thing he'd love to leave me out of and tell me about later.

Oh, Annie, he'll say, you should have been there. It was unbelievable.

I turn sideways and slide into his room so I don't have to open the door any farther—otherwise, Creak City.

It's dark in here. No moonlight filters through the shut blinds. Takes my eyes a second to adjust.

Then I see him.

Stuart's in bed. Asleep.

Okay, I was wrong. Good. Now I can go back to bed and—

Behind me the closet door squeaks open.

So it wasn't Stu I heard moving around in here! It was—

I freeze as a dark figure lunges at me from the closet!

# CHAPTER 2

**B**EFORE I CAN SCREAM, MY ATTACKER STOPS MY mouth with his black-gloved hands. My heart stops, too. I can't believe what I'm seeing. It's—

*Stu?*

He's dressed in a black turtleneck and black parka and a black knit ski cap and puffy black ski gloves. He presses down hard on my mouth. "You going to be quiet?" he whispers fiercely.

Quiet? I'm too scared to breathe. I nod, but just barely.

"You going to scream or do anything stupid?"

I shake my head, and he lets go.

"Oh wow," I whimper. My whole body feels light, like somebody removed the bones.

Anybody would be scared if somebody dressed all in black leaped out at them from the closet. But with me, I'm extra scared.

See, there's something I haven't told you about.

Alston Manor.

Alston is the suburb of Baltimore where Stu and I live. (We've only been here six months. Dad changed jobs—*again*.) And Alston *Manor* is the joke name people use for the prison. It's out by Alston Mall and Playland, the big amusement park.

This prison—it scares me *so* much. I won't go to movies at the mall, even when something really good is playing, because it's right near the prison.

Alston Manor is a big brick building that looks so solid an atom bomb couldn't budge it. On all four sides looms this tall electric fence with barbed wire and little gray guardhouses on each corner. At Alston Manor, they keep the lights on all night. In every cell, all night long, a naked bulb burns. Stu says that's so they can check to make sure the prisoners aren't trying to escape.

Escape.

What if one of those convicts got out? Stu says no one could ever break out of Alston. But what if someone did? What if he came to my house?

I know that's unlikely. But when I saw Stu leaping out at me just now, all dressed like a criminal? It was my first thought, I'm not kidding.

"What are you doing?" Stu demands, his voice pained and high.

"What am *I* doing? You try to strangle me and give me a heart attack and you ask what *I'm* doing?"

Stu smiles nervously, then starts pacing. "What are you doing in my room, is what I mean. I mean, how many times have I told you. . . . ?" He sticks his head out into the hall, then comes back inside and goes back to pacing.

"I—I wanted to see what *you* were doing," I say.

"Shh," Stuart warns, taking a giant step toward me. I didn't mean to, but I guess I raised my voice. He glances toward the door. Listens until he's sure

Mom's not up. Then he shakes his head and laughs a little. "You really scared me," he mutters.

"I scared *you*?"

Then it hits me. If Stu was hiding in the closet, who's in the bed? I whirl.

A sleeping bag and some shirts and a pillow, that's who.

I stare at my brother.

"You're . . . you're going out," I say.

"Duh, Sherlock," Stuart cracks. "Now go back to bed."

He takes a step toward the door, but I grab his arm and hang off it. "Where? Where are you going?"

He swings me once, then pries off my fingers. "Let go!"

"Mom will kill you," I warn. "She will kill you dead and eat you for breakfast."

This is true. Lately, Dad's been away on a ton of business trips. He sells computer chips to companies all over the country. At least he tries. Tonight he's in Idaho, I think. Anyway, with Dad away so much, Mom's been acting like she's both our mom and our dad. She makes up all these new rules, like no TV on school nights, and she grounds us whenever we slip up.

Stu says, "Mom's not going to kill me, 'cause she's not going to know. Now come on, Annie, out of my way, I'm in a big—"

"Just tell me where you're going," I beg, my voice rising into a squeal.

I don't know what it is about older brothers. Whenever I'm around Stuart I act younger. I get all whiny. Which makes Stu want to be around me even less. But I can't help it. Right now I feel about ten instead of twelve, and my age is dropping fast.

"Okay," says Stu, "if I tell you where I'm going, will you go back to your room and go to sleep and promise me on your life a million times that you won't tell—"

He stops short. I can see in his eyes that he knows he just made a mistake.

"I won't tell Mom," I tell him, grinning slyly, "if you take me with you."

Stu grins back, but not like he thinks I'm funny, more like he has gas pain. "No way."

"Puhlease?"

Now I feel about six years old. At this rate, in about two seconds I'll have to put on diapers.

"Look, I'm just going to hang with some kids," Stuart says. He pulls back one glove and wipes sweat from his forehead with the back of his hand.

"Hang?" My eyes bug. "At *midnight?*"

Stu chews on his chapped lower lip, which is a bad habit he has. "Stop it," I tell him. He stops. "*What* kids?"

"What difference does it make?"

"*What kids?!*"

"Dave Blackstone."

He says this in this offhand way, out of the side of his mouth, like it's the sort of thing that happens every day.

"Dave Blackstone?!" I gasp.

"Shhh!"

"Since when are you friends with Dave Blackstone?"

Dave Blackstone is fifteen like Stu. Only difference, Dave's one of the coolest kids in town. Part of that is 'cause Dave's dad *owns* Playland. I mean, can you imagine? Every kid wishes his dad would get him a great toy. Dave's dad bought his family a whole big amusement park! They can probably go to Playland anytime they want for free.

I don't ever want to go to Playland myself, of course, but that's another story. And I don't want to get into it, if you don't mind. But—

Dave Blackstone!

If you've ever been to Alston, you've seen Dave's picture for sure. Dave's father, Harvey Blackstone, has these billboards that show his whole great-looking blond family standing in front of Playland under a caption that reads FUN FOR THE WHOLE FAMILY.

Playland may be fun for the whole family, but Dave Blackstone only hangs out with a few other really cool kids.

"I didn't even know you were *talking* to Dave Blackstone," I say. Then my jaw drops. 'Cause I'm remembering. After school today I tried to get Stu to bike home with me and I saw him talking to Dave and his girlfriend, Cassandra. Stu waved me away like I was a mosquito buzzing in his ear.

"Is this what you were talking to Dave about after school?"

"Annie, trust me on this. You would not want to go where we're going, *okay?*"

Which of course makes me want to go a hundred times more. "Try me," I say.

Stu pulls back his glove and peers at his watch. He gasps. "I gotta fly. Go back to bed, kiddo."

Kiddo. I hate it when Stu calls me nicknames like that. I like it, too, but mostly I hate it. From the time I was six until I was nine Stu could make me have a total screaming hissy fit by calling me "honeypot." So of course he called me honeypot every chance he got.

See, back then I wasn't so stick thin like I am now. These days I've been shooting up. I'm only one inch shorter than Stu. But back then I was short and a little bit chubby.

Stu tries to worm past me, but I block his way. "If you go," I threaten, "I'll wake up Mom."

Stu turns red. "Annie, I'm warning you. You blow this for me and—and—"

"And what?" I say, shoving out my jaw.

"And I'll never let you sit with me during lunch break. Think about it."

I think about it.

Alston High is right next to the middle school, where I go. Sometimes after I finish eating lunch I look for Stu and stay with him until the bell rings for fourth period.

We've only been in Alston six months, like I said. Stu says the reason I haven't made more friends my age is that I'm always asking kids what they're doing and then asking if I can join them, and then pleading with them and begging them to let me join them, just like I do with Stu. He says that you have to act more standoffish.

I don't know. Whenever I find Stu during lunch period he's almost always by himself. So it's not like *his* strategy is working so beautifully.

"If you let me come, I'll do you a favor," I offer. He rolls his eyes. "A big favor," I add.

"No."

"Two big favors."

He doesn't bother to answer, just shoves me aside and hurries out the door. I stand there watching him tiptoe fast down the front steps.

Going, going, gone.

Well, no way, Stuart Blake.

You're not leaving me out this time.

I run down the hall to my room, running on tiptoes so I don't make too much noise but—

Oh wow, I just lost my balance and—

I'm going to crash right into Mom's door!

You know what? I came *this* close to hitting the door. I stand here, heart pounding. If I wake up Mom and she catches Stu, she'll kill him. And you heard Stu. If I get him in trouble, he'll freeze me out, even more than usual.

I listen hard to the sounds from behind Mom's

door. Awesome luck. There's no sound at all. I didn't wake her.

*That* close to the door, I'm telling you.

I tiptoe into my room. Gotta fly. No time to get dressed. I pull my denim jacket off my desk chair—

Whoops. Almost pulled the desk chair over with a crash.

But I caught it in time. I sling the jacket over my white flannel nightgown, the one with the little blue umbrellas floating all over it (it's one of Mom's old nighties, and it's about ten sizes too big for me, but I love it). I pull a red ski cap over my long auburn hair. Then I yank my ratty old black high-tops onto my bare feet and head for the door without even tying the laces when—

Mom's bedroom door flies open. And Mom comes out.

# CHAPTER 3

I BACK INTO MY ROOM SO FAST. ONE HUGE GIANT STEP like I just got blown backward in an explosion.

Did she see me?

Yes! Yes! She's turning toward my room. She's coming this way!

And then . . .

She strides right into my room, and comes right over to me. She puts her face only a few inches from mine.

I can feel her warm breath on my cheek.

I'm dead.

## CHAPTER 4

**B**UT HERE'S THE LUCKY THING. BEFORE MOM CAME into my room, I dove into bed and pulled the covers over my denim jacket. I got my ski cap off and jammed it under the pillow.

Now I keep my eyes shut tight. While she studies my face I try to breathe deep and slow, instead of fast and shallow like I'm choking to death, which is how I feel.

After a few seconds Mom leaves. Fooled her! Yes!

Uh-oh. Mom's going down the hall to check on Stu.

It's not my fault, Stu. She's going to catch you, but it's not my fault. Oh, right. Like Stu will believe that. I'm dead. I'm dead I'm dead I'm dead I'm—

Wait a second. Here come the footsteps again.

So Stu's pillows-and-clothes-in-the-bed trick worked on Mom, too!

Mom doesn't bother about which floorboards she

steps on. *Creak creak creak.* Hey, when you're a grown-up, you can step on any board you like.

She listens outside my door, then goes back in her room and—

Closes her door.

I can't believe what I'm thinking. No, Annie. No way. I mean, don't push your luck. Wherever Stu went, he's long gone. You'll never catch him. You'll only get him in trouble and get you in trouble and—

Then I think about Stu hanging out with Dave Blackstone.

I don't get it. Overnight my unhappy geeky brother turns into Joe Cool from the In-Crowd. You know how that makes me feel? I'll tell you how that makes me feel. I feel like, if I let Stu go out without me tonight, I'm going to get left out for good. 'Cause if Stu's IN, then I've got no one to be OUT with, if you see what I mean.

"Okay," I say in the tiniest of whispers. "Here goes."

I slowly push down the covers, swing my sneakers down to the floor. I pull my ski cap back on, tossing the long tail over my shoulder.

Then it's back to tiptoeing and studying floorboards. I'm so quiet Truman doesn't wake up when I walk right past his wet black nose.

Not that Truman is some kind of guard dog. Truman's a cocker spaniel. He's fifty-nine (in dog years) and he's always been way overly friendly, so that everyone but me tries to push him off their lap and out of their face.

If a convict did break out of Alston Manor and came to our house? Truman would slobber all over his black gloves.

I go out the front door into the chilly fall night. I turn and slowly push the door shut behind me till it latches with a tiny click.

Which is when I realize.

I didn't bring my key.

I just locked myself out.

Excellent. I shiver on the porch. If I don't find Stu, I'm dead meat a million times over. I turn my head every which way.

No Stu. No nobody. No nothing.

Dead meat, here I come.

Next to me are houses identical to mine and across from me are more of them. Some are gray, like ours. Some are painted other worn-out pastel colors. But basically all the houses are the same— big and dark and ugly. Like a herd of sleeping cows.

We live in Hilltop Village. It's this small housing development built on top of a small—you guessed it—hill. It's a pretty lonely place. Only about half the houses have people in them. That's because right after the developers built Hilltop, the city built a new highway. The new highway bypassed this whole area. So Hilltop is no longer such a desirable spot to live. The owners keep lowering the prices, which is how Dad could afford it. But nobody moves in.

I fly down the walk, then start running across the cold dewy grass. Hurry, Annie. Hurry!

The wind blows hard into my face, like it's trying to hold me back. Why didn't I dress more warmly? What if I have to sit on our porch for hours waiting for Stu to come home?

"Stu?" I whisper fiercely.

No answer. Just the hum of the big metal streetlights that line the walks. My heart sinks even lower.

It's so strange being out this late. I feel like I'm awake but in a dream. Except I can see my breath plume out of my mouth. And as I run the cold air cuts my lungs. So I know this is real. And a real nightmare unless I—

A shadow darts behind a house.

Oh, please! I follow the shadow, running harder. As I come closer the shadow stops and spins to face me.

"What are you doing?" Stu demands angrily.

I'm too out of breath and happy to answer. I just hug him.

"Get off. Are you nuts? What are you doing out here?"

"I'm coming with you."

*"What?!"*

We're standing right next to somebody's bedroom window. We're making a lot of noise, too, but luckily this is one of the many houses that isn't sold or rented.

I hate these empty houses. They're creepy. With no curtains, the windows get this empty dark look like eye sockets in a skull. I cup my hands around my eyes and try to look inside. Same as our house, except no furniture, no pictures on the walls, no nothing. Creepy.

Stuart points back home like I'm Truman or something. "Go home!"

"I'm not a dog," I point out.

Hey, if he's going to treat me like Truman, then I'm going to follow his orders just as well as Truman would. So when Stuart starts off again, I follow about five yards behind him. He keeps turning and pointing for me to go back. No way. I'm starting to like this game. Maybe I'll run and chew on his ankles.

Finally, over by the tennis court, Stuart stops and waits for me to catch up.

"Look," he says, "I don't even know if these guys are going to let me go with them. They said *maybe*. You understand? But if *you're* there—"

"Oh, that's nice," I say.

" 'Cause you're younger," he adds quickly.

Younger. That's right. I'm younger. And I always

will be. When Stuart was twelve, I used to think that was just about as old as you could get. Now it seems like nothing, 'cause he's fifteen. Fifteen!

Stuart stalks off across the tennis court. I run after him, the long tail of my ski cap flapping against my back. We enter the last courtyard of Hilltop, where there's one more semicircle of houses. These are the last houses before you get to the Model House. Then there's the guardhouse and the entrance gate.

Breathing hard, Stuart stops and leans against the back of a house, right next to a tightly coiled garden hose. "Annie," he says, his voice full of pleading, "I gotta sneak past the guardhouse. This is no joke. I can't sneak you. I don't even know if I can make it alone. Look how you're dressed. That white nightie."

"So?"

"Don't you see? You're going to mess me up. You're going to ruin everything."

"Three big favors," I offer.

Stuart sighs. He bites his lower lip and stares up at the clear night sky, like he wishes the Man in the Moon would speak to me and make me go back home.

"Okay," he says finally, giving me this brief phony grin.

I can't believe I heard right.

"*Okay?* Okay I can come?" I almost shout for joy, but I remember just in time that we have to keep quiet. I hug Stuart again. He pushes me away.

"Yeah. For three big favors, you can come."

"Deal."

We do our secret shake. Stuart made it up. You lick the back of your hand, wave it over your head all goofy, then you do a high five and slide through a low five.

I feel so excited. Stuart looks happy, too. Could

that mean maybe he secretly kinda sorta wanted me to come along?

Probably not. But—

Wait a minute. WAIT A MINUTE!

Stu's letting me come with him!

Now what did I get myself into?

# CHAPTER 5

WE SNEAK ALONG THE GRAVEL DRIVE THAT LEADS TO the guardhouse. Up ahead, there's one last house off to the side, all by itself.

It's the Model House, which I believe I mentioned. It's the house the Hilltop owners fixed up extra special to show what you can do with your house if you buy one.

They show the Model House to all the people who are thinking about moving to Hilltop, of which lately there have been none. They showed it to us when Dad took us to check out Hilltop.

It's like a ghost house. There's furniture, a few old magazines fanned out on the coffee table, shades on the windows (which are open day and night). For Halloween last week the owners even stuck these two cutout figures in the bedroom window, just to be cute.

Yup. See? Still there.

I hate the Model House. It gives me the same fake feeling I get from all of Hilltop Village. Like we all just pretend to live here.

Stu puts his hand on my shoulder, stopping me.

"What?"

"We gotta be real careful, Annie. From now on the guard can see us."

"Really?"

I feel like I'm in a spy movie. Like we could get shot at any second, and the whole world depends on our getting across enemy lines. It's scary, but at the same time it's fun, because I'm with Stu. And we're not really doing anything so terrible, right? After all, we do live here. The worst that could happen is that the guard catches us and tells—

Mom.

Come to think of it, we're in a very bad situation.

"Okay," Stu says, "we're going to have to crawl." He lowers himself to the ground.

Crawl?

"Are you insane? Stuart, the drive is all gravel."

"You want to go home?" he asks, without looking at me. "Be my guest."

That was mean. I look down at Stu for a second, trying to think of a mean thing to say back. Instead I flop down next to him.

"Okay," Stuart says, "head for the Model House."

We crawl across the gravel on our bellies. And right away I get scratched all over my shins and my palms and my belly and my face, like I'm a giant chalkboard and every stone signs its name on me and—

Uh-oh. I stop crawling and grab Stu's arm. He turns and looks at me, saying "What?" with his eyes.

Up ahead I can see the guard in his little guardhouse. The guardhouse is all lit up in the darkness, like a TV playing in the middle of a dark room. The guard wears a green uniform and green cap like a policeman. He's got his head down, reading a paper. He's not looking our way. But he will be looking our way in about two seconds unless I can find some way not to—

Cough. Here I go. Can't help it. I only cough twice, two sharp coughs to get it over with as fast as possible. But right away I see the terror in Stu's eyes and then—

The guard turns his head and looks—

Right at us.

## CHAPTER 6

**1** STARE DOWN AT THE GRAVEL.

You're a rock, I tell myself. You're not here.

When I look up again, the guard is back to reading his paper.

We're safe!

Stuart doesn't look scared anymore. He looks furious. I shrug my shoulders a little (it's not easy shrugging when you're lying down) as if to say, What can I do?

Then Stu starts crawling again and I follow him and we make it—behind the Model House. We lean against the wall, catching our breath.

Now what? The Model House stands about twenty yards from the front gate. And for those twenty yards we'll be out in the open and right under the guard's nose.

Well, don't worry, Annie. Stu's a genius. He must

have figured this out. He must have an incredible plan. "So what's your plan?" I ask.

"I don't have one," Stu says, without looking at me. He sneaks a peek around the corner of the Model House.

"You don't have a plan?!"

I can't believe it. Stuart is winging it! Here I felt safe knowing Stu was in charge. But Stu has no idea what's going to happen next!

The guardhouse is a little white building like a miniature house. It guards the entrance gate, which is the only way in or out of Hilltop. There's a big fence around the whole village like a prison. Only this fence is meant to keep people *out,* not in.

The entrance driveway has big wooden crossbars like a railroad crossing. The guard has to raise the crossbars up and down when you want to drive in or out.

I know what you're thinking. With all this security, why do I worry about escaped convicts?

You know how it is. When you get scared about something, you can say a hundred different reasons to yourself why you shouldn't be scared, and it doesn't do any good.

But I'm letting my mind wander. We need a plan!

I stare past the guardhouse. From up here you can see little parts of the road that runs below the hill and—

Is that . . . ?

Yes—there's something moving down there. A big blurry shape. A car. With its lights off. It turns up the long drive to Hilltop. And all of a sudden I've got it.

"Stu."

"What?"

"Look."

Stuart looks where I'm pointing. Then his head jerks forward slightly and I know he sees the car.

"Perfect," he says. He grabs my arm, squeezing hard. "When the guard checks that car through, that's when we'll sneak out," he whispers in my face. I can smell his breath. In between meals, Stu's breath always smells like peanuts.

"Once we're past the guardhouse, turn left into the bushes," Stu rushes on. "We'll crawl through the bushes. Stay close to the fence until we're out of sight of the guardhouse. Then we'll go down the hill. You got it? Annie, listen. This is important. Are you listening?"

He's acting like it's his plan, not mine. But I don't want to make him mad. So "Got it" is all I say.

The car heads up the hill. Now the guard puts down the paper and moves to the window on the IN side of the guardhouse.

"Now!" whispers Stu.

We start to run.

# CHAPTER 7

**A**S I RUN I CROUCH. I DON'T KNOW IF THIS MAKES IT harder for the guard to see me or not, but I can't help it. It's like instinct, my body's way of saying PLEASE DON'T LOOK AT ME!

The guard raises the IN crossbar. Then he comes out of the guardhouse on the IN side and says "Hey" to the driver of the car, like he knows him. Then he glances in back of the car as—

Stu ducks under the long white splintery crossbar on the OUT side of the driveway.

He's under, through, safe.

Now me.

I duck down under the crossbar and head after Stu, except—

My big billowy nightgown catches on the splintery wood.

I pull but—
Oh no!
I'm stuck!

# CHAPTER 8

STU TURNS, LOOKING BACK AT ME IN AMAZEMENT. HE waves hard for me to come on. I yank with my whole body but—

Feels like the splinter drives deeper into the folds of my nightgown, holding me tight. I wave at Stu. He rushes to help.

I can hear the guard on the other side of the guardhouse, chatting with the driver. "You have any trouble?" he asks.

Oh, yeah, I've got trouble. Big trouble.

"Not so far," says a voice.

"Good," says the guard.

I hear the car drive through.

Which means I've got about two seconds before the guard comes back in the guardhouse and maybe one more second before he sees me. I reach behind me, trying to find where the nightgown is caught. Stuart grabs my nightgown and pulls. But we're both in each other's way and frantic and we're fumbling and not getting me unstuck as—

Somewhere down the drive I hear the car park. A door opens. Shuts. Footsteps crunch over gravel.

"Annie!" Stuart whispers in my ear. "The car! It's—"

He doesn't finish. He doesn't have to. I hear the tires scrape. I see the car coming. Back. Headed toward the OUT driveway. Headed—

Right at us.

# CHAPTER 9

THE CAR DRIVES CLOSER, CLOSER.

But I'm stuck to the crossbar. Pinned to the wood like a worm on a hook.

I grab the crossbar with one hand, and with the other hand I grab a hunk of my nightgown and pull with all my might.

*Rippppp!*

You know what? I think I just ripped my nightgown to pieces but—

I think I'm free—

Yes! I'm—

The crossbar lifts me straight into the air.

# CHAPTER 10

WHEN THE CROSSBAR STOPS GOING UP, I'M HANGING by one arm. Ten feet off the ground. I flail my legs. I feel the cold wind blow on my bare calves.

Through the window of the guardhouse, I can see the top of the guard's green cap. He watches the car as it—

Heads toward the entrance gate, picking up speed. Still with its lights off. So it won't be able to see me when I drop down right in front of it and—

Hold on, Annie!

I grip the wood with all my might, but I can feel my fingers slipping as—

The car zips underneath me.

That's some relief. Now when I fall I'm only going to bash my brains out against—

Oh—

I'm—
f
a
l
l
i
n
g

**C**HAPTER
**11**

**T**HAT'S THE STRANGEST THING. I DIDN'T FALL. I MEAN, I did fall, but the moment I fell, it was like I was already standing on the ground.

I get it.

As I lost my grip the crossbar came back down! So by the time I let go I was on the ground again!

Ha-ha! Amazing!

The guard in the guardhouse is watching the car disappear down the drive. Then his head moves. Down. He's back to reading his paper. But—if he looks up, we'll be staring right into each other's eyes.

Stu rushes out of the bushes. I'm too stunned to move. He has to pull me into the bushes like we're playing football and he's tackling me.

Then he has to pull on my arm to get me moving. We crawl through the bushes. We stay close to the fence, just like he said.

There's not a lot of room back here. Little branches snap me in the face. But as I crawl I begin to calm down.

We made it.

WE MADE IT!

I can't believe it. I feel like jumping up and down and shouting and clapping. But first things first. Right now we have to crawl. And crawl. Up ahead, Stuart giggles like a maniac. What's so funny?

I guess I must have looked pretty funny hanging off the crossbar, dangling way up in the air, kicking my legs back and forth. When I picture it, I laugh, too.

"Hey," I whisper, "you said you wanted to hang out."

He snort-laughs. And soon, even though we keep shushing each other and trying to hold it in, we're laughing hysterically. I clench my jaw shut, but it doesn't help. We stop crawling and for a while we just laugh. Finally Stu stops laughing enough to say, "Okay, we better hurry."

We start crawling again.

After a while I notice that along with being excited and still having the giggles, I'm also cold and exhausted and sweaty and I'm grinding dirt and bark and twigs into my skin. I also remember how close I came to getting seriously hurt when I was caught on the crossbar.

"Stuart?"

"Yeah?"

"Let's go back."

"What do you mean?"

"Let's go home."

There's a long pause. Maybe he's going to say, Sure, okay.

Please say, Sure, okay.

"Annie, we can't just go back, you know. I mean, we have to sneak past the guard again, remember?"

He's got a point.

"Look," he whispers, "I'll tell you what. If you want to stay here, I'll come get you in a couple of hours. But you can't move, okay?"

Oh, yeah, wonderful. I really want to lie in the shrubbery all night waiting for Stuart. Though I have to admit, I consider it for a second.

"You going to stay?" he asks.

"No," I say into the ground.

"Okay, then let's go."

He stands up. We wade through the thick bushes and come out on the sloping grass of the hill. We run. Except the hill is so steep it feels more like we're falling.

There's a little road at the bottom of Hilltop Village. Nothing much. Stuart runs across the road without looking. Mom and Dad have screamed at him about this his whole life, and a couple of times he's almost gotten himself run over and killed.

Stuart's always been what Mom and Dad call a problem child. He goes out of his way to do really bad things. Like once he smoked a cigarette in his room. Mom went ballistic when she caught him. Screamed and cried and said he was going to kill himself. I cried, too, as a matter of fact, just from the thought of Stu dying of cancer. I know one cigarette won't do that to you, but it was such a sad and awful thought.

Me, I never cross a street without looking both ways. Tonight I look both ways more than once, even though it's the middle of the night and the road is totally deserted. The car that nearly ran me over as it drove out of Hilltop is long gone. I guess I'm stalling.

Why?

Hey, Annie, it's just a road. Piece of cake after hanging from a crossbar.

But crossing this road, it feels like the point of no

return. 'Cause now that we're out of Hilltop, Mom will really kill us if she catches us.

I don't know what I was thinking when I insisted on coming with Stu. Did I think Dave Blackstone was going to come to Hilltop and hang out with us on the tennis court?

On the other side of the road, Stu turns to look for me. When he sees I'm still standing back on this side of the road, he throws his gloved hands up in the air. Then he turns and stomps into the woods.

He's not waiting.

Oh, boy. Here we go.

I cross the road.

# CHAPTER 12

AFTER WE HURRY THROUGH A PATCH OF WOODS, WE come out on Dunbarton Oaks Road, which is also deserted. We walk along the side of the road for a while, kicking up leaves. Amazing. Here I am. Annie Blake. Out in the middle of the night. I let out a whoop.

"Quiet!" orders Stu.

"Sorry."

I throw my head back, staring up at the curved glass bell of the sky, with all the shiny pinholes that are stars.

I don't know about you, but I've always been pretty scared of nighttime. And the thought of being *outside* at night used to petrify me to death. I don't know what I figured it would be like. I guess I thought that the only people who went out at night were escaped convicts waiting to strangle you.

Instead, it feels calm and peaceful. Like the whole

world is sleeping, even the leaves and the ground
and the road and—

"Annie! Duck!" cries Stu, pulling my arm.

And the next thing I know we're both diving down
alongside the road as—

A cop car cruises slowly by.

"Did they see us?" I ask.

Stu doesn't say anything for a sec, just keeps
watching the dark road. "I don't think so." He gets
back up and wipes leaves from his black parka.

You know what? That was kind of fun. Diving for
cover, I mean. Here I've always been scared of escaped convicts. Now it's like Stu and I have escaped
from Hilltop Village, and the cops are out looking for
*us*!

"This way," Stu says.

"Where are we going, by the way?"

"You'll see."

We go through a place in this big metal fence
where the bars have been bent back and we can slip
through. And the next thing I know we're tromping
along vast fields of short green grass all silver in the
moonlight. Which is when I figure out where we are.

The Alston Public Golf Club. During the day, kids
like to sneak in here and hunt for lost golf balls.
Stu's got two bucketsful in his closet. I've hunted a
little, but I've never found a ball. Stu says that's because I stay by the fence. Which is true. The thought
of some golf ball zinging me is, well, extremely un-
pleasant.

Well, that's one thing I don't have to worry about
right now. Getting hit. Not too many people play golf
at midnight.

The grass feels wet and spongy. Dew soaks my
sneakers. Then I see it. A spot of white. A golf ball! I
run over to the white spot.

"Annie, come on! I'm late," Stuart calls.

"But I found a—"

I found a piece of a white foam coffee cup. Not a golf ball at all.

"Come on!" Stuart snaps.

I trudge over to Stuart. I've got my head down. Disappointed, I kick at a little white rock. Which rolls.

"Stu! Look! I found one! I found a golf ball!"

I show him. The ball says ARNOLD PALMER in black script. How do you like that? Some guy took the trouble to print his name on the ball and then he lost it. Hooray!

Stuart grins, picks up the long tail of my ski hat by the little red pom-pom, then drops it again. "Nice going. Come on."

As I walk I unzip my jacket. Except the zipper sticks, as usual. And when I get the jacket open, I get even more chilled by the wind than I was a second ago.

I button the golf ball into the breast pocket of my nightie. Then I fumble with the zipper of my jacket with thick, frozen fingers for about thirty yards before I get it closed again.

But my whole mood is going up, up, like that crossbar back at the guardhouse. We snuck out of Hilltop. I found my first golf ball. Stu's being nice to me. Nothing can go wrong now.

It's my lucky night.

# CHAPTER 13

"SO COME ON, STU, TELL ME WHERE WE'RE GOING."

We've reached the driveway that leads out of the golf course, and we're climbing over another set of crossbars. Metal ones, this time. Even though there's no guard, and I know these bars won't go flying up in the air, my heart beats a little faster as I swing my leg over the cold metal. Stuart catches my eye, and we both laugh, remembering.

"I said, where are we going?" I ask.

"Playland," Stuart says.

I gape at him so long I have to run to catch up with him as he lopes down the club's long driveway. I know I didn't hear right. If I had heard right, I'd be very upset and very scared. But I know I didn't—

"Playland?"

"Right."

Right. My worst nightmare. Just like he said.

*Trust me, Annie, you don't want to go where we're going.* Now, why didn't I trust him?

"We're going to Playland *now?*"

"Yeah."

As we reach the road Stuart picks up a wet stick and starts banging tree trunks as we walk.

"Stu, I hate to break it to you, but Playland is closed. Closes at ten."

Actually, I'm very glad to break this to Stu. Because I gotta tell you, Playland is like the last place on Earth that I want to go. I don't even like going to Playland in the daytime!

For one thing, it's near Alston Manor. For another, the only rides I feel safe on at Playland are the kiddie rides, which you can't be caught dead on when you're my age. And then they've got this monster roller coaster—

"Stu, stop teasing."

"I'm not teasing."

He's not teasing.

Oh boy.

At Playland, there are a lot of awful wicked horrible rides. Rides that spin you, pull you, twist you, turn you, bump you, and whip you. Rides designed to make you throw up every bit of junk food they just sold you. (I guess they want to empty out your stomach so they can sell you more junk food.)

But the scariest ride by far—

Is called—

The Serpent.

I've never been able to get up the courage for that thing.

It's a roller coaster with three giant loop-di-loops that take you totally upside down, so that your insides probably fall right out, let alone your lunch.

And . . . well . . . I guess I might as well say what happened.

I was in Playland two months ago on a birthday-party outing with some girls from my class. I was so excited to be invited. Though I think that only happened cause Mom met Suzie Elmont's mother in the supermarket and twisted her arm.

At the time I didn't care. I was just so happy to be part of it. But then—

This is really embarrassing, what I'm about to tell you.

When all the girls went on the Serpent, I chickened out. You can imagine the way the other girls made fun of me for that, but I couldn't help it. I just couldn't ride the Serpent. I couldn't.

The girls kept teasing. I started crying. Mrs. Elmont had to drive me home.

That was, I have to say, pretty much the low point of my life to date. I've tried hard to forget it. But every time I so much as hear the word *Playland,* the whole scene instantly replays in my mind like I swallowed a giant TV.

"I *know* Playland is closed," Stu says. "Dave's father owns the place, remember?"

"So what?"

"So Dave knows where his dad keeps the keys. And sometimes he and his older brother, Hal, go there at night and have the whole place to themselves. Neat, huh?"

I'm going to throw up.

"They sneak in? Isn't that dangerous?"

Stuart snorts. "Yes. That's the point, Annie."

Do you understand this? Risking our lives—this is the point? What point?

"Anyway," Stuart says, "tonight"—he breaks his stick over his knee—"tonight they said they might— they *might*—let me come with them."

And this is the night I had to tag along. This is the time I had to be the big buttinsky. I could have stayed in bed. Toasty warm and sound asleep. But noooo.

Then I think of something that makes me feel a whole lot calmer.

"Stu, do you know how far Playland is? We can't walk to Playland, it'll take all night."

"We're not walking to Playland, doof. We're walking to Dave's house."

"Dave's house? We're going to Dave's house?" I'm so nervous I have to repeat everything Stu says. "And then what?"

"Dave's older brother has a car."

Dave's fifteen. Hal's sixteen. So he might have a license. But if Mom has one rule above all others, it's that we're not allowed to be driven around by anybody without her specific permission.

Stu stops, turns, puts his hand on my shoulder. "Annie?"

"Yeah?"

He frowns. "It was stupid of me to let you come."

"No, it wasn't. What are you talking about? Get off."

Stuart studies my face like he's trying to see if I'm going to cry. I stick out my tongue.

"I tried to talk you out of it, remember?" he says.

Sounds like he's preparing his case for when Mom and Dad have him arrested for taking me out at night.

"Let's go," I say angrily, trying to sound all brave.

"Okay, but look, if you want to go back, just say the word, and . . . I'll take you back. I'm serious."

I guess it's nice of Stuart, offering to take me back. That would ruin his night. But it makes me furious. I tromp on ahead, down the road.

He treats me like a baby. Baby sister. That's one of his stinko nicknames. Well, I'm no baby. I'll show him. I'll ride the Serpent. I'll ride it with no hands. I'll ride with no legs. I'll ride with no body because I CAN *NOT* RIDE THE SERPENT. I can't! I can't!

Well, maybe I won't have to. Maybe something will come up.

Like what?

We trek along a bunch of streets before we come to streets with houses on them. We're not saying much. Until I say, "What do you care so much about hanging out with these kids, anyway?"

It's a mean thing to say. At least I hope it is.

"I mean," I go on, "why do we have to go through all this trouble just so you can hang with some idiot kids from your class?"

"I don't care so much about being with them," Stu insists, which is a big lie. I can tell by the frown on his face.

"You do."

"Don't."

"Do."

"Don't."

You know how I said I get younger around Stu? Same thing happens to him, come to think of it.

We start across a lawn, headed toward this huge sprawling white clapboard house. Looks mega-fancy. There's a separate garage and a pool (it's covered with a tarp) and a gazebo. Stu doesn't have to tell me. This is the Blackstone house.

I glance at Stu. "Okay, genius. How do we wake up Dave without waking up his dad?"

"His dad's out of town on a business trip. Just like our dad."

Business trip. What gives with these dads? Seems like that's all they do, go away.

"What about Mrs. Blackstone?"

"She went with him. They left Hal in charge."

Stuart's got that smirk, like he's thought of everything. Makes my blood boil. Why can't he be scared like me?

I start off ahead of him, as if I know where I'm going, which I don't.

Stu grabs my shoulder, spinning me around. "Hold up. Time for the first big favor."

"What?"

"You owe me three big favors, remember?"

I glare at him. Why did I agree to three big favors? That was so dumb. But it's done. "Shoot," I say.

"You can't say anything."

I feel the tips of my ears start to burn. "What do you mean?"

"Starting right now and all the time we're around Dave and Cassandra and Hal. You can't say a word. You can't open your mouth. Not once. Got it?"

"You're out of your mind."

"First big favor, Annie. You don't have a choice. You have to let me do all the talking. All of it. You get me?"

I'm so angry. Stu acts like I'm a mess-up who'll just cause trouble. I mean, okay, I was the one who got stuck on the crossbar but—

Aw, I don't even want to think about it. "Okay," I say.

"Uhn-uh," Stu says, smiling and shaking a finger in my face. "I said you can't talk. Now try again."

I scowl at him furiously, but I don't open my mouth.

"Good," Stu says. "You got it now?"

I open my mouth. I'm about to say that of course I've got it, but I stop myself just in time.

"Very good," Stu says with a big grin. "But I better give you a harder test . . . honeypot!"

My eyes pop. My fists clench. But somehow I manage to keep from shouting.

"*Very* very good," Stu says, "I'm impressed. Now remember. The whole time we're with them."

Hey, no prob, Stu. Believe me, I'm not so eager to talk to you at the moment. He thinks that honeypot business is a joke. Some joke. I'll show him. If he calls me honeypot just a few too many more times, I'll—I'll—

What will I do?

I'll do him the favor of not speaking to him for the rest of my life, that's what!

Stu leads us around to the back door. Which is a lot fancier than the *front* door at our house. The big black door has a brass lion's-head knocker. Stu lifts the brass ring in the lion's mouth, drops it. *Clang*—

No response.

He slaps his black gloves together and blows steam like a scared horse. "Great," he mutters. "You made me miss them. Great, great, great."

He knocks a few more times, waits, listens. Nothing. Then he turns and stares back across the lawn, anger and frustration twisting his features together into a big knot.

Oh, right. This is just another thing I did wrong, making us late. Hey, Stu, I can't talk, so I can't tell you this, but I'm glad you missed them. Ha-ha-ha. Serves you right.

It also means I don't have to ride the Serpent!

That's good news, and a big relief. But I can't even look at Stu, I feel so lousy and angry and hurt at the way he's treating me. So instead I stare past him at the door as—

The door opens.

I don't say anything.

For one thing, I'm not allowed to say anything, you know, 'cause of Big Favor #1.

For another thing, I'm way too scared.

Standing in the doorway is a tall cop with a pair of handcuffs in his hand.

"Stuart Blake?" he says.

Stu spins, gasps.

"I just got a call from your mom, Stu," says the cop, dangling the cuffs in our faces.

"Mom called?"

"That's right. Your mom says she wants me to

teach you a lesson about sneaking out at night. So . . ."

The cop reaches over and cuffs my wrist with Stu's.

"You're under arrest," the cop says.

# CHAPTER 14

Stu and I stare at each other. Our mouths hang open.

Under arrest?

"That's right, kiddies," says the cop, who looks oddly familiar. "You're going straight to Alston Manor."

Ohhhhh—

My worst nightmare!

"Oh, please," I beg, and I can't even hear what I'm saying after that 'cause Stuart's begging right along with me, so our pleas mix together into one garbled stream of pleading and—

The cop throws back his head and roars with laughter. "Hi," he says when he finally stops guffawing. "I'm Hal, Dave's brother. Come on in. Dave's expecting you."

Dave's brother? Hal? I can't think straight. Does that mean we're not under arrest?

"You like my cop costume?" asks the cop—I mean, Hal. As he leads us inside a marble foyer he tips his hat. "Got it for Halloween."

Hal, Dave's brother. I knew he looked familiar. Now I know where I've seen him. On the billboard. The Playland ad. All the Blackstone kids have short blond hair. Hal's the tallest gangly blond kid, the one with a pointy chin.

There are also three Blackstone girls. The oldest, Liza, is my age. She was at that party at Playland where I—well, you remember. I sure hope she's asleep. Everyone from that party loves to giggle when they see me.

"This way," says Hal the cop.

In the middle of a huge fancy living room with a marble floor and marble pillars, Dave Blackstone lies sprawled out on an endless leather sofa. He eats Cheeze-ums from a jumbo-size box and watches *Letterman* on a projection-screen TV. He whoops when Hal tells him the story of how scared we were. Stu and I stand with our heads slightly down and our wrists cuffed together.

Dave's shorter than Hal, but stockier, more muscular looking. His face is wider, his features are bigger. He's also about six times better looking than Hal. I feel like I'm meeting a movie star or something. In fact, you know what? I think Dave is so handsome I wish I could be him, even though he's a guy and I'm a girl. That probably sounds idiotic, but it's the way I feel.

Hal disappears into the kitchen. I hear him rustling around in there. Dave keeps watching TV like he forgot we're here or something.

I look at Stu. He watches Dave. He looks so polite and respectful. Which is I guess how I look, too.

Then a toilet flushes somewhere and Cassandra comes in. Forget about being Dave. I want to be Cassie. She's got red hair down to her waist in back.

And the way she shakes her head when she walks, she's like a beautiful pony. She flicks us a glance with her almond-shaped green eyes, then strolls over to the sofa and curls up next to Dave.

They kiss.

Right in front of us.

The handcuffs jerk against my wrist. I glance at Stu, who stares at Dave and Cassie, looking all tense. He must be nuts with jealousy. You know how I said he doesn't have a mess of friends? Well, of the friends that he does have, none of them is a girl, let alone a girl as beautiful as Cassie.

Dave pushes Cassie away. She says, "Hey." She says it gently, though, like she's afraid to get him mad.

"Look who's here," Dave tells her, like she didn't see us.

"Hi," Cassie says. She looks at us blankly.

All of a sudden I feel sorry for Stu. Here he thought he was going to hang out with these guys. Standing in the corner handcuffed to his kid sister— that couldn't be what he had in mind.

Dave remotes the TV off, stretches, yawns. "What'd you bring *her* for?" he asks Stu.

It takes me a second to realize he means me.

"I couldn't help it," says Stu, his voice sounding high. "She followed me."

So much for feeling sorry for Stu. I have to bite my lip to keep from growling. What he said is true, okay, but still—did he have to say it? Right in front of Dave and Cassie? I want to yell at him, but I can't 'cause—

Big Favor #1.

"Come on," Stu says, "open these cuffs. I already got her glued to me, I don't need her cuffed to me, too."

Now I really hate Stu. It's one thing to treat me like this in private, but . . .

"Sure," says Dave. "Hal!"

Hal sticks his head in from the kitchen. He munches on a handful of pretzel bites. "What?"

"Uncuff them," Dave tells him. The way he speaks to him—it's more like Hal's the younger brother. I wonder how Dave pulls that off. Someday I'd love to try.

Hal stuffs all the little pretzels into his mouth at once, then reaches his hand in the trouser pocket of his cop uniform. He looks surprised. He chews, swallows, then reaches his hand in the other trouser pocket. Then he starts in on the buttoned front pockets of his blue cop shirt.

He starts to panic. But not as much as I am. I'm starting to sweat.

"You didn't lose the key, did you?" Dave demands. "Tell me you didn't lose the key, Hal."

"I—I—I lost the key," stammers Hal.

# CHAPTER 15

**M**Y JAW DROPS. HE LOST THE KEY. STU AND I ARE handcuffed together for life.

Well, at least this will make it easier for me to tag along.

Then Dave cackles. And I finally realize—

They're just teasing. They have the key. Except—

Cassie slinks off the couch, and as she slips on her suede jacket she says, "If you want to come with us tonight, Stu, you have to wear the cuffs. Those are the rules."

"Aw, come on," Stu says, but he sounds polite and respectful when he says it.

"Those are the rules," Cassie repeats with a little smile. "I thought you said you wanted to join us."

"I—I did," agrees Stu. "I do."

"And today at school you said you could handle anything, remember?"

"Yeah. Of course I can."

I gawk at him. I've never seen Stu act like this. So desperate to please. What happened to his whole philosophy of being standoffish?

I mean, can you believe it? Stu's just like me! He wants in just as badly as I do!

"Okay," Dave says, yawning, "we're outta here."

Here we go. Showtime.

Everyone heads for the back door, with me and Stu sort of shuffling since we're cuffed together. Then Cassie says, "Dave, the hamburger."

I have no idea what she's talking about, but it terrifies me. Right now everything terrifies me.

"Right, thanks," says Dave. "Hold on." He runs back into the house, comes back a moment later with a shrink-wrapped package of raw chuck chop from the supermarket.

Now what is *that* for?

No thanks, Dave, I'm not really hungry.

Then we all file back across the lawn to a black BMW. Black, like a hearse. And suddenly I realize it's now or never. I've got to put my foot down. I stop short. The cuffs bite hard into my wrist—because Stu keeps going. Then he comes back, glowering at me in the darkness.

"What?"

"I'm not going," I say. "You're not going, either. You know what Mom says. We don't have permission to ride with Hal."

"Oh, please."

"I'm serious."

Stu pulls on the cuffs, hurting my wrist even more. "Hey," he says. "No talking, remember? Favor number one."

"The favors are off."

"What?! Annie, listen. We snuck out of the house. I mean, now is not the time to start worrying about

Mom's rules. We're already breaking all the rules, kiddo!"

Dave and Hal and Cassie climb in the car, Hal behind the wheel, Dave and Cassie in back. They leave the front door open for us. A window powers down. "You coming or not?" Dave calls out.

"I'm coming!" Stu insists.

I keep thinking about the way Stu acted in the living room. Complaining about having to be stuck with me all the time.

"Go ahead," I hiss at him. "You go if you want to go so much. Go suck up to the cool kids. I'm staying right here."

"Don't be a jerk!" Stu growls, turning red.

"*You're* being a jerk."

"Shut up!"

"You shut up."

I can hear Dave and everyone laughing in the car. I don't care. Well, I guess I do care, 'cause my heart pounds like crazy.

"Just go!" I say. My voice chokes. "You said I could go home if I wanted to. Well, now I want to. Don't worry. I'll get home okay."

"Without me," Stu says.

"Yeah."

"You can't go without me."

"Oh, don't start acting like you care," I spit out. "I saw the way you acted in there."

"Guys?" Dave calls. "Sometime in this century?"

"Just one sec," Stu turns and pleads. Notice how his voice turns all nicey-nice when he talks to Dave. Then he spins back and talks to me in a fury. "Annie, I didn't ask you to come here. I didn't ask you to come and ruin my life! If you go now, I go, too."

"Why?"

"WHY?"

Stu raises his wrist high, which means my hand goes straight up in the air like I want the teacher to call on me. He rattles the cuffs.

"Now, are you going or not?" he demands.

# CHAPTER 16

I GO.

Dave, Cassie, and Hal laugh the entire time. No matter what they say they seem to think it's hysterical.

Hal drives. In his cop uniform. So among other things I have this nightmarish feeling that we're getting driven to Alston Manor. Playland is right near the place, remember?

Handcuffs are a major pain. Every time I want to do anything simple such as blow my nose, Stu and I have to go through this whole big maneuver.

All my life I've heard about kids going out for late-night joyrides. I guess this is what they're talking about. Except, where's the joy part? I must be missing something.

We're not wearing our seat belts. Another thing Mom would kill us for. But hey, Annie, look on the bright side. She can only kill us once.

By the way, I'm back to doing Big Favor #1. Haven't said a word since we got in the car. Cassie even says, "What's the matter with your sister, Stu? Doesn't she know how to talk?" She leans over the seat and nudges me. "Don't you know how to talk?"

I don't answer. I keep my eyes on the road.

"What do you got," Dave chimes in, "glue on your tongue?"

Oh, clever. Glue on the tongue. Sheer genius.

You know what? This not-talking business has its advantages. I don't have to bother trying to come up with a snappy comeback. I can just sit here and sulk and try to show Stu what a bad time I'm having and make sure he knows that it's all his fault.

Only problem, Stu's not looking at me.

Only other problem—

Hal drives awful fast. But Dave keeps telling him to go faster and not drive like a dweeb. And Hal does it. He steps down on the gas and drives even faster.

We whip around sharp corners. I brace myself against the seat. I clutch Stu's hand, but he shoves it away. Except he can't get my hand away from his, thanks to the cuffs.

"Yo, slowpoke," Dave calls to Hal, "don't you see the road is deserted? Move it."

Faster.

I feel like I'm in a video game, only I'm the little monster who's going to vanish with a little bloop-bloop sound effect when we bash into something.

What am I saying? This isn't a video game, and this isn't a roller coaster. If we bash into something—

Lucky thing the road is deserted, just like Dave says. The dark woods fly past us on either side, but there are no cars coming the other—

HONK!

S C R E E C H!

Whoa.

A car just came out of nowhere and flew right past us, headlights burning my eyeballs, horn screaming in my ears.

Hal hit the brakes so hard I thought Stu and I were going to go right through the windshield. I mean—

That—was—close!

So what does Hal do? He goes right back to speeding. The needle flicks up to—

SEVENTY MILES AN HOUR!

Hey. Remember that cop car? When Stu and I had to dive to the side of the road? What if Hal gets a ticket?

You know what? At this point that would be the greatest thing in the world. Because even though we'd be caught, the nightmare would be over. The cops would take us home, we'd get screamed at and grounded for like infinity, but at least we'd be safe and not speeding down a lonely road and—

ABOUT TO HIT A TREE!

Hal swerves just in time, fishtailing through the gravelly shoulder of the road. "Fast enough for you?!" he shouts back to Dave.

"No way!" Dave yells. "What is this? A kiddie ride?"

I start wishing for a cop car with all my might.

Then I let out a little gasp.

A cop car. Coming toward us. It's like I have magic powers. Like I wished this cop car into life.

"Slow down, Hal," Dave warns from the backseat. "What are you going so fast for?"

As if he wasn't the one who's been telling Hal to hurry it up.

Hal slows down. But it's too late. The cops are going to pull us over.

Yes!

Hey . . . wait!

The cops wave and smile and drive right by.

**CHAPTER 17**

**D**AVE AND HAL AND CASSIE GUFFAW AND SLAP EACH other on the back. Stu laughs, too, but more like he wants to play along than he really thinks it's funny.

Me, I'm in shock. Why did those cops let us go? Hal was doing seventy in a thirty-mile zone.

Then I get it. And I get the joke, too. Hal's uniform. They thought he was a cop.

We drive past Alston Mall. It's small, with all the stores in one long strip. It's also one of the many places around here hit hard by the new highway bypass. Out of the whole long line of stores, only two places are still in business. There's Kazam—the magic store where Hal probably got his cop costume and cuffs. And there's the Alston Duplex, the movie theater.

Both Kazam and the Duplex are closed for the night, so the mall looks even more deserted than usual. Hal cuts through the parking lot, bumping hard over the curb. Our tailpipe scrapes loudly, and we all scream.

You know what this is like? It's like we're already on the Serpent. Headed for the first loop.

I feel a cold blast of air as Dave powers down his window. "Hey, Dad!" he yells, leaning out and waving. "How ya doing?"

Dad? Mr. Blackstone is out here in the middle of the night?

Then I see what Dave means. He's waving at the big Playland billboard that marks the turnoff to the amusement park. I stare at the painted faces of Hal and Dave. Strange to see them smiling at me ten feet high when I'm here in the car with them.

"Nice to see you for once, Dad," yells Dave, "you bum!"

Cassie and Hal laugh. Stu laughs, too, but I wonder if he really gets the joke. I don't.

"What's the matter, Dad? Don't you have anything to say?" Dave yells at the billboard as it disappears into the night.

Hal takes the next turnoff, the one with the giant clown pointing the way—to Playland. Hal turns so fast, the tires screech.

"What a bum," Dave mutters.

My face has gone stiff. What's with this bum business? I mean, I get mad at my dad sometimes, but I would never—

"Dave hates Dad," Hal explains to us, smiling. "Don't you, Dave?"

"Yeah," Dave agrees sourly.

"Gee, Dave," says Hal, "why don't you just tell Dad how you feel?"

"If he was ever around, I would."

"Why do you hate him?" I ask, forgetting my promise to Stu, who pulls hard on the cuffs to remind me.

"Hey, Dave?" Hal calls, taking his eyes off the road

as he looks at his brother in the rearview. "The girl wants to know how come you hate Dad."

"Because he's a bum," Dave explains.

Cassie laughs and hugs Dave, like no matter what he says it's wonderful.

"Dave's just sore 'cause Dad cut off our allowance," Hal explains, looking past Stu to me.

"That's not why," says Dave. He turns and stares out the window at the darkness as if he's trying to hide his face.

"Sure it's not," says Hal.

"It's *not*."

"Business at Playland hasn't been so great lately," Hal tells me and Stu, "in case you hadn't noticed."

Just then, something inside me gets all tense, like my body knows before I do that we're passing—

I turn. Sure enough. There's the big brick building.

Alston Manor. Where a naked bulb burns in every cell. I glance at Stu. Stu knows how much I hate this place. He gives me a little reassuring smile. I stop hating Stu, at least for a second.

Then Dave says, "Okay, Hal, pull over."

Hal jams on the brakes. Dave leans over the seat and pats me on the back. "Get out," he says, smiling. "Both of you."

"What do you mean?" asks Stu. Beads of sweat pop out on his forehead, like extra pimples. I'm sweating, too.

"Which word don't you understand?" Dave asks. "Get? Or out?"

Cassandra giggles.

I look at Stu.

"You didn't really think we'd let you come with us," Dave says, "did you? Get real, geek. You fools are going to Alston Manor."

## CHAPTER 18

**D**AVE DIVES OVER MY SHOULDER AND THROWS OPEN the door. At the same time Hal turns and starts bunny-kicking Stu with his sneakers as he shoves us both out of the car.

"Out!" yells Dave.

I put one sneaker out onto the ground. I'm shaking all over. Then the car takes off again, with me sitting half in and half out. I have to lean way back in or fall right out of the car.

Stu helps pull me back inside, then leans across me and gets the door closed. "Funny," he tells Dave and Hal. "Very funny."

I can't believe I'm not sobbing. I really can't. Under the circumstances, this feels like a major accomplishment.

Dave and Hal and Cassie are all back to laughing.

Come on, Stu. Tell them off. Tell them!

But instead Stu starts laughing, too!

Well, I don't laugh, believe me.

Alston Manor.

It takes me a while to stop shaking. I stare out the windshield so I don't have to look at anyone.

Then I see it.

Up ahead.

Playland.

Playland is one of the largest amusement parks in Maryland. If you spent a whole day here, you'd probably only hit half the rides. It looks like a whole city unto itself.

Like Hilltop, and like Alston Manor, Playland has a big fence around it. There are night-lights, plus moonlight, making the whole place look silver and weird. The big ugly metal rides stick up into the sky like a crowd of giant robots and monsters.

Want to hear something that always really creeps me out about this place? Playland is so close to Alston Manor, they say that during the day the convicts can hear kids screaming and laughing on the rides. Don't you think that's completely eerie?

Right outside of Playland there's this huge—and I mean huge—parking lot. But like Hal said, Playland hasn't been doing so great lately. So usually the parking lot isn't full.

Well, in the middle of the night? It's totally empty, a sea of black pavement with little white lines all over it.

Hal drives around the parking lot in big circles. Dave opens all the doors. Hal spins the car around and around as they all laugh and hoot and holler.

At least *they're* having a joyride, even if I'm miserable.

Hey, no, you guys are right. Driving in circles sure is fun.

Just think: These kids are older than I am.

Finally Hal drives across the huge parking lot and

up to the giant metal entrance gates that lead into Playland. The gates are closed and—

I just had a beautiful thought. Maybe Dave's key won't work in the lock. Or maybe this was all another trick to scare us. I would like that. I would like that very much.

"You got the keys?" Hal asks Dave.

Dave leans over the seat and dangles the keys next to Hal's face.

So much for that little daydream. We all pile out of the car. Except me and Stu; since we're handcuffed, we have to go slow.

"Okay," Hal says when we're finally out. "I'll be back in like an hour."

"You don't want to come with us?" Cassandra asks him.

"Yeah, Hal," Dave jokes, "Playland's fun for the whole family, dude."

Hal grins and drives off, slapping the outside of his car door once by way of good-bye.

Good-bye. Now if only Dave and Cassandra would go away and Stu and I could go home.

Instead, we head for the entrance gate. From here I can see the big Ferris wheel, the bumper cars, the top of Nightmare Mountain, and—

Rising high above the whole park—

Shiny and menacing in the moonlight—

There's—

The Serpent.

I've got a riddle for you. What's three hundred feet tall and goes upside down three times?

I didn't make that riddle up. It's from the TV ads for Playland. In the ad, the kid gets the answer wrong, and then he screams like a maniac as he rides the Serpent roller coaster and it plunges straight down at a million miles an hour.

The Serpent. The biggest, baddest roller coaster of them all.

Just as long as they don't make us go on that.

"You like the Serpent?" Dave asks me, following my gaze.

I gulp.

"I hope so," he says, smiling sweetly, "'cuz you guys are going for a ride!"

My STOMACH DROPS DOWN INTO MY HIGH-TOPS. I can already feel the little car whooshing me around the tracks. Dropping me fast. Taking me through the loops. And in the dark, no less. Oh no. Oh no oh no oh no oh no.

Dave glances around, peering into the darkness, like someone might be spying on us.

Could we get arrested for breaking into the amusement park when it belongs to Dave's dad?

I figure no, but I'm not sure, so it's just one more thing to worry about.

Dave steps up to the big wrought-iron gate and fumbles with the keys. He sticks one of the keys into the lock.

The gate has the word *Playland* woven in metal inside a big circle at the top. On top of each spike of the fence stands a giant cartoon animal figure—a bunny, a bear, a frog. In bright sunlight these animals look friendly and happy. In the moonlight, they look like crazed psycho killers.

Maybe the keys won't work. Please don't let the keys work. Please don't—

"Huh," says Dave. "Weird. Gate's already open."

He turns and gives us a puzzled look.

"You sure?" Cassie asks him.

"Yeah."

He pulls the big gate shut an inch, then pushes it open again, like he can't believe it. "See? Open."

"What does that mean?" asks Cassie. "That it's open." She sounds a little worried.

Great. Now even the big kids are worried.

"It means the idiot guard who locked up tonight must have messed up big time," Dave says, still studying the gate.

"You should tell your dad," I say helpfully.

Stu glares at me.

"How can he tell his father, goofhead?" says Cassie. "We're not supposed to be here, *remember*?"

Boy, am I sorry I opened my mouth.

Dave takes out the package of raw hamburger, rips off the shrink-wrap, which he tosses (that's littering, but I'm sure not going to open my mouth again). Dave starts kneading the hamburger between his hands.

I forgot about the hamburger.

Now, what is that for?

"What's that for?" Stu asks.

"What's what for?" Dave echoes.

Stu's got this smirk on his face like he couldn't care less, which I know is a bluff. He's probably getting as worried as I am. "What's that hamburger for?"

"This?" Dave asks.

Have I mentioned that I don't want to be Dave anymore? Not even if I could look like him. I mean, I hate kids who repeat your questions like that. They know what you mean, but they try to make you ask your question at least twice so you feel real stupid for asking.

"This is for the Dobermans," Dave explains casually.

The what?

Hello!

Did you hear what he just said?

I glance at Stu.

'Cause maybe Stu will still be smiling. That will show me that I don't have to have a heart attack and die.

Stu's eyes are wide and dark with fear.

"Dad's got three guard dogs," explains Dave. "Rudolph, Prancer, and Dancer."

Well, they sound cute, anyway. Aren't those three of Santa's reindeer?

"Dad lets the dogs roam around the park loose at night." Dave chuckles. "They'll probably tear us to pieces."

He makes a fist. Raw meat oozes between his fingers.

Good night.

"Yeah, I wish I could see the look on Dad's face," muses Dave, "when they tell him it was his own guard dogs that chewed me up. Won't Dad feel sorry for me then."

Cassie runs her hand through Dave's short blond hair, like he's this hypersensitive guy we all have to take care of. I'm not worrying about Dave's feelings at the moment. I'm worrying about those dogs.

Dobermans. Not cocker spaniels. Attack dogs that have been bred through the centuries so that all they think about is how to kill and maim and chomp down on your throat.

Then Dave grins. "Just kidding. The dogs know me. And they know I feed them. That's why I always bring hamburger. Hey." He glances at Cassie. "I wonder—"

"What?" I ask. Let Stu glare at me, I can't help it. I've got to talk.

"The gate was open," muses Dave. "I hope the dogs didn't get out."

He looks at us for a second, thinking, then shrugs. He swings open the metal gate. *C-r-e-a-k*. He lobs in the hamburger and quickly pulls the gate shut.

We all wait. My eyes stick to the hamburger like glue. I'm listening for those dogs with my whole body.

Then I hear a snarl.

As a Doberman clamps its sharp teeth on my bare leg!

# CHAPTER 20

I SCREAM. THEN I SEE WHO IT IS. CASSIE. WITH HER long red sharp nails, pinching my leg. Laughing. Dave's laughing, too. At least Stu's not laughing. I'll give him that.

"Come on," Dave says, pushing open the gate. He picks up the pile of hamburger and squishes the whole thing into the front pocket of his gray Alston High sweatshirt.

"So that was all made up about the dogs, right?" I ask.

"What?" Dave says. "Oh, no. The dogs are real. I made up the part about the gate being open, just so Cassie could really freak you out when she grabbed your leg."

He glances around, listening. "The dogs will be around," he promises me.

Something to look forward to.

We head into Playland. We walk along these

smooth rolling trails of black pavement. Past the fake trees and the fake boulders and the fake grass. Right away we come to the big gingerbread house of a ticket booth. The windows are locked shut. We climb over the metal turnstiles. More crossbars.

You've been to a big amusement park, right? It's fun. It's exciting. They've always got all this music playing. Crowds stream in and out. Jolly people wander around in big funny costumes giving out free balloons. That kind of thing.

Going into an amusement park, that's always been the best part for me. Within a couple of hours I'm exhausted and burned by the sun and bored and sad and disappointed and I want to puke from eating too much carmelcorn and cotton candy and ice cream.

But going in . . .

Has never been as thrilling as this, let me tell you.

I feel like I'm entering another planet. And at any moment aliens could jump out and get us.

Only these aliens are dogs.

We go past the empty bandstand where during the day a woman tries to guess your age and if she's off by two years you get a prize.

Past all the colorful signs advertising the different concessions, games, and rides. The concessions are all boarded up, just like the ticket booth.

This is worse than those empty houses back at Hilltop. This is like a cemetery. A cemetery of a place where people used to have fun.

There's the merry-go-round. Strange. At night, even the kiddie rides look freaky. Look at the open mouths of those horses. In the dark, my eyes play tricks on me. I could almost swear those horses watch us as we walk by.

We pass the baby roller coaster where a couple of cars go around a small railroad track in a circle. Why couldn't they let us ride *that* and call it a night?

"You guys want to go down the water slide?" Dave asks.

He can't be serious. The water slide has no water on it. They don't run it this late in the season. It's bone-dry. A big giant blue monster sticking up into the night sky. Speaking of sticking, if they make us go down that thing, we'd freeze and stick to the metal.

"No, please," I murmur.

Dave and Cassie laugh. As they walk on ahead of us Stu mutters, "Don't show them you're scared. Just relax."

Relax?

"Just try to have a good time."

Oh, right. Cuffed to Stu in Playland in the middle of the night with three rabid dogs on the loose. He's right. I wonder why I can't just relax and have a good time?

"If they see you're scared, they'll pick on you more," Stu explains out of the side of his mouth. "They're bored, that's all. They're just trying to amuse themselves."

"Well, they've come to the right place for it," I joke.

Stu doesn't laugh. I think he's pretty tensed up himself.

"Just relax," Stu whispers nervously. "Lighten up. You look like you're going to pass out."

"Can't help it," I say cheerfully.

"Try."

But you know what? A strange thing begins to happen.

Not all at once. But . . .

We start going on the rides. Starting with the bumper cars. Dave and Cassie bash into us from both sides. But still, nothing bad happens. Kind of fun.

Then we go on these high-backed saucer seats

that whirl you. I used to hate these, but tonight they don't seem so awful for some reason.

And here's the strange thing that's happening. I'm actually starting to relax and have a good time. Dave and Cassie and Stu shout like kids do at amusement parks. I shout some, too. And—

I gotta admit. It's kind of great having the whole amusement park to ourselves. No long lines, right? Seriously, that's mainly what you do at amusement parks. Wait in lines and argue with your brother until your parents start yelling at you for being un-grateful 'cause hey, they took you to the park.

Dave has master keys that turn on everything. Which is a cool feeling. We own the place.

And the more time that goes by without anything awful happening, the more I start to believe that nothing really bad *will* happen.

Then things get even better. Dave lets us into one of the game arcades, and we play Skee-Ball. I have to shoot rightie, since my left hand is cuffed to Stu. Well, maybe I should switch to being right-handed, 'cause I land the ball in the hundred-point hole three times in a row! And Dave lets me keep all the little prize tickets that come spitting out of the ma-chine. He says I should save them and cash them in when I'm here during the day.

Cassie pats my head through my ski hat. "Nice shooting, kid," she says.

She grins. I grin.

You know what? I don't even mind being called kid, I'm feeling so good all of a sudden.

"Who's thirsty?" Dave asks, when we're back out-side the arcade.

Turns out we're all thirsty. Dave leads us over to a boarded-up food stand and fumbles with the keys.

"You'll love this," Cassie says. "You can have any-thing you want."

Seems like Cassie and Dave are actually starting to like us.

I can't help it. Even though I decided that I'm not all that crazy about Cassie and Dave, it feels so great, being liked, by Dave and Cassie of all people!

They're not so bad after all. Hey, they were just in a bad mood before. Which I can understand. I mean, Dave's dad doesn't give him an allowance and is never around. I know how that feels.

And they're hanging out with me. Me, Annie, a mere twelve-year-old. Oh, if only the girls from my class could see me now!

Dave disappears into the concession booth.

I give Cassie a big grin as—

Three Dobermans come around the corner of the concession stand and run right at us!

# CHAPTER 21

STU AND I SCREAM. SO DOES CASSIE. WE ALL BACK UP. Stu and I fall over in a heap, and I think I just broke my arm as—

Here come the dogs.

Sleek brown-black dogs with silver-studded collars and wet sharp teeth. The dogs leap around me and Stu, barking, snarling, drooling, sharp teeth bared!

We try to get up, but with our cuffs on, we get twisted like a pretzel and go down again.

I catch a glimpse of Dave as he runs out of the concession stand with two huge sodas, which he drops on the ground.

Stu and I are raw meat.

The dogs are going to chomp down on our throats!

# CHAPTER 22

"**R**UDOLPH! PRANCER! DANCER! OVER HERE! SEE? Food!"

It's Dave, yelling. But the dogs keep their jaws open, ready to chomp our throats out. Then they look up.

Dave holds out the hamburger. Dangles it. "Hungry?" he yells.

He throws the hamburger. As soon as the hamburger lands the dogs pounce, fighting each other, jockeying for position. Growling, snarling, and barking, the dogs devour the meat as—

Stu and I roll to safety.

We get up and do our shuffle-run over to Dave and Cassie. Then we all just stand there, watching the dogs eat. That's the way they would have eaten me and Stu, in one more second.

"They're not as vicious as they seem," Dave promises us. He looks genuinely sorry.

Thanks a lot.

"They wouldn't have really hurt you," he says.

Uh-huh.

The dogs finish their treat. I flinch as they trot back over to us. But Dave scratches them behind the ears and pats them and they seem happy, even friendly. Then they walk off, like they have business to attend to. So long, guys. See you on the roller coaster.

Dave takes us inside the concession stand and pours everyone sodas. No one says a word. We all gulp down the drinks. We litter the empty cups. Then Dave locks the booth and says, "Okay, let's go."

"Wait."

It's Stu. He sounds angry.

"Yeah?" Dave asks.

"That's enough," says Stu.

It's about time! Stu's finally going to stand up to him! Go, Stu!

"That's enough? What do you mean?" Dave asks, squinting.

"You said you wanted to give me a little test," says Stu, "you know, to see if I could cut it. Well—the dogs. That was enough. Now I'm in. Uncuff us. I've got to take her home."

By "her" he means me.

See, there's something I forgot to mention.

I'm crying.

Can't help it. Been doing it since the dogs—

Those eyes. Those teeth. So close!

"Sorry," Dave says. "No can do. You gotta ride the Serpent, like I told you."

Tell him, Stu. Tell him off!

"Aw, come on," Stu pleads.

Pleading? That's not what I had in mind. I had in mind for Stu to do some insisting and even some yelling and maybe even some punching if it came down to it.

"Hey, Cassie rode the Serpent in the dark for me," says Dave. "Didn't you, Cassie?"

"Sure did."

"Otherwise I'd never go out with her," explains Dave with a grin.

"Hey." Cassie punches his shoulder. He slaps her fist away, laughing.

Don't give up, Stu, I silently beg. Talk Dave out of it.

"So," Dave says. "It's up to you, Stu-man. If you want to take the test and ride the Serpent, that's cool. If you don't want to, that's cool, too. Your choice, pal."

"I want to ride it," Stu says, "but let my sister go. That's all I'm saying."

Right then I forgive Stu for everything bad he's done to me. (At least, stuff he's done tonight. I'll never forgive him for all those times he called me honeypot. Never.)

I stop crying, mostly, as I wipe my eyes with my right hand.

In a way, I'm glad I cried. Now I've sunk as low as I can go. It's like, okay, I got that out of the way. Now it's time to grow up. I want to leave this crying business in the dust, if you know what I mean.

"That's okay," I say. "If Stu rides, I ride, too."

Stu looks amazed. He gives me a little smile. Teensy. But I can tell he's impressed. I give him one back.

"Okay," says Dave with another shrug. "Then let's go."

# CHAPTER 23

**T**HEY MARCH US THROUGH THE PARK LIKE PRISONERS going to the electric chair in Alston Manor. Not that Alston Manor has an electric chair, but you get what I mean. Me and Stu up ahead. Dave and Cassie about ten yards behind, whispering and laughing.

We keep seeing signs. Big clowns whose large red hands point you to the various rides. Now that I said I would ride the Serpent, I figure my only hope is that we get lost for hours, until the park opens in the morning.

Fat chance. The Serpent is easy to find. It rises higher than anything else in the park.

We don't have much farther to go. Right past the Tilt-o-Whirl looms the entrance to . . . the Serpent.

"Okay, Cassie," Dave tells her, "you set them up in one of the cars, I'll open the booth."

You know how when you've been dreading something, it makes it even scarier once it finally happens? Well, I've been dreading going on the Serpent ever since we moved here. And ever since that horrible birthday party, I've been dreading it ten times worse. And then, ever since Stu told me we were going to Playland tonight, I've been dreading it a hundred times more and—

I'm no math whiz, so I can't do the arithmetic. But you multiply all those dreads and you know how I feel. Like I'm about to faint.

Cassie leads us through the endless winding ramps that lead to the loading dock. Usually the ramps are clogged with people waiting to ride. Even though Playland isn't doing well, the Serpent always does good business. During the day it's a half-hour wait, minimum.

What I wouldn't give for a half-hour wait.

"Tickets," Cassie says when we get to the track.

We look at her stupidly.

"Just kidding. Lighten up, guys. It's only a coaster. You're not really this scared of a ride, are you?"

"We're not scared," Stu says grimly.

We. I like that. I like that a lot.

The cars that ride the Serpent come in chains. There are fifteen small cars in each chain. With snake designs painted all over the outside plus a snake's head with a forked red tongue on the front car.

All along the loading track, there are large signs with warnings painted in big red letters.

WARNING!

NEVER REMOVE SEAT BELT OR SAFETY BAR WHILE RIDE IS IN PROGRESS.

KEEP YOUR HANDS IN CAR AT ALL TIMES.

NO GUM CHEWING.

EMPTY YOUR POCKETS BEFORE GOING ON RIDE!

At the bottom there's one more instruction.

Note to operators: Fill cars from middle of chain first!

I study the rules, reading them over and over again.

"Here," Cassie says, leading us to the front of a snake chain. "Get in."

"Hold up," Stu says, grabbing her arm.

Cassie pulls her arm away fast. She glances nervously toward the control booth. "What are you, insane?" she murmurs.

What? If Dave sees Stu even touch her arm, Dave will go psycho or something?

As if we don't have enough problems.

"Look." Stu nods at one of the warning signs. So I guess he's been checking them out, too. "It says load from the middle first. That's to keep the chain balanced on the loops."

Remember how I told you Stu was this math whiz and science genius? It may sound like nothing much, but I think this is a good example of how smart he is. I just read that sign ten times, but I didn't really understand what I was reading. Stu read the sign once and knew exactly what it meant.

"Oh, yeah," Cassie says, peering at the sign. "I guess you're right. Good point."

"I thought you rode this thing before," I can't help saying.

"I did." She smiles. Girls who are this pretty, they know they can get away with anything. No matter what happens, they just smile.

"Come on!" Dave calls from the booth. "Let's go!"

"Hold on." Stu gives Cassie his keys. "Check your pockets," he tells me.

I check. Nothing but my prize tickets. I keep those.

Stu studies me. "You sure?" he asks.

He means, am I sure I want to ride the Serpent. I've never been less sure of anything.

"Uh-huh."

"Okay," Stu tells Cassie. "We're ready."

To die.

Cassie helps me as we climb into the middle car of the chain, which isn't so easy when you're hand-cuffed to your brother. She has to help us on with our seat belts. As she latches my belt she whispers, "You probably shouldn't be riding this thing at all."

Couldn't agree with you more. But what does she mean? My left eye starts twitching.

"What do you mean?" asks Stu.

Cassie lowers the safety bar, locking us into place. I feel the cold bar press down against my nightgown and my thighs.

"The Serpent shorted out today," she explains, still keeping her voice low. "They didn't let anyone ride it this afternoon. They said it's got to be worked over. I told Dave we should cancel this trip but—"

"Cassie!" shouts Dave. "You ready or what?"

Stu and I stare at Cassie in horror and disbelief as—

Cassie backs up and yells, "Okay. We're ready."

"Wait a sec," I say. But my mouth has gone as dry as the water slide and I can't make the words come out.

And then the car jerks forward and—

It's too late.

We're off.

# CHAPTER 24

THE LONG STRING OF CARS RISES SLOWLY. SLOWLY.

*Clickety-clack, clickety-clack.*

Up the giant hill.

We're rising at such a steep angle that I'm pressed back against the metal seat.

Up ahead the track stretches endlessly, like a ladder to the stars.

Three hundred feet.

And you know what? I've been through a lot of scares tonight. Real scares, not the fake ones a roller coaster is supposed to give you. You would think that after hanging off a crossbar or speeding in Hal's car, a roller coaster would be a piece of cake.

Nope. That's the news, folks. Those other scares don't help at all. This coaster? It feels like the scariest scare I've ever faced.

*Clickety-clack, clickety-clack.*

Sounds like someone's winding us up. And then

they're going to shoot us to kingdom come, which is basically what the Serpent does, when you think about it.

Don't think about it, Annie. Look somewhere else. Unglue your eyes from the endless track and—

Wow. Look at that. Who knew we were already up so high! We can see out over the park. And you know what? Maybe I better keep my eyes on the track after all, because that way I can't really tell how high we're—

Ohhhhhh. Now I can see out over the big fence around Playland. Out into Alston.

What a lovely view. Why, there's Hilltop Village! Good-bye, Mom. Good-bye, Truman. Don't mourn for me too long.

As much as I try to hold it in, I let out a whimper and lean my head on Stu's shoulder. I made a terrible mistake. I should never have volunteered for this ride. I would like to go back now. Can I go back now? Guess not.

"Thanks," I mutter into Stuart's parka. Then I straighten up.

"For what?"

We're both looking straight ahead. Kind of a strange way to have a conversation.

"For telling them to let me go," I say.

"You okay?"

I don't even answer, that's how unokay I am. And Stu doesn't ask me again, so he's probably not so okay either. What happens if the whole ride shorts out like it did this afternoon? That's what I want to know. But I'm afraid to ask that out loud. If I open my mouth, I might throw up.

"Close your eyes," Stu suggests. "It might make it easier."

It might, except here's the problem. My eyes are already closed. And the ride feels worse with my eyes shut. I get this awful seasick feeling of rising in

the darkness and not knowing when we're going
to—
   I open my eyes.
   AYYYYYY!
   I scream at the top of my lungs as—
   We plunge down down down—
   Into the dark.

# CHAPTER 25

WE ZOOM DOWN THE FIRST HILL. I SCREAM MY HEAD off. My teeth rattle. My skull rattles. My whole body rattles.

Whenever you see kids on the roller coaster, they have their hands up in the air. Look, Ma, no hands. Well, forget it. Not me. I'm squeezing the safety bar for dear life. I keep screaming as the coaster takes us through these—

AYYYY!!

Sudden twists and—

AYYYY!

Hairpin turns and—

HERE COMES THE FIRST BIG LOOP AND—

WE'RE UPSIDE DOWN!

My ski hat flies off as—

Oooooooo—

All my organs smush up toward my head—

But then, just when I think I can't take it anymore—

We're right side up again, and my organs fall back into approximately the right places and—

I'm okay I'm okay I'm okay! But—

Here comes the SECOND loop and it's bigger than the first loop and—

"STU!" I scream. "I CAN'T TAKE IT!"

"HANG ON! YOU'LL BE FINE!"

Wow. We were upside down for a lot longer that time. Couldn't talk. Couldn't think. Just had to suffer through it.

You know how I thought I couldn't take that loop? I was right. I can't. I mean, I'm still here, but at the same time it's like I'm gone and—

Ohhh. I think I did throw up. Hmm. I hope it landed right on Dave and Cassie.

I mean, can you believe kids pay to go on this thing? Well, hey! We get to ride for free. What a treat.

*Clickety-clack, clickety-clack.*

I really hate that sound. 'Cause it's the sound the cars make as they slowly—

Yup. We're going up again. Isn't this ridiculous? The ride's taking us up just so it can drop us again. Why do they have to drag it out this way?

Note for the files: Someday I must design a better ride. I'll call it "Instant Death." You won't feel a thing. And it'll all be over in one second. Hey, if I had to choose between that and the Serpent, it would be no contest. Instant Death all the—

"Only one more loop!" Stu yells at me.

One more loop? Yup. He's right. You don't have to be a genius in math to do this arithmetic. The Serpent has three loops. We've been on two so far. That means we're headed for—

The biggest loop of all!

# CHAPTER 26

NO, NO, NO, I CAN'T TAKE IT, I CAN'T TAKE IT, I—
I close my eyes.
I clench my teeth as—
We spin upside down for a third—
We're upside down, zooming along, endlessly, endlessly, endlessly—
My mouth drops open in a silent scream when—
What was that? That crackling sound.
Was that . . . ?
Could that have been . . . ?
Sparks?
But—wait!
Feel that?
Yes! Yes! I think—
The ride's over!
Oh, oh, oh—just when I thought I couldn't take it anymore, the ride is finally ending because—
See, the car slows down, glides forward, then

back, then forward, less and less distance each time
until—

We're dead still.

I'm. So. Happy.

But . . .

Hey . . .

How could . . .

The ride be over so fast?

I mean, the last thing I remember we were in the
big huge awful final loop.

But come on, Annie. Good news is good news,
right? Why fight it?

I open my eyes.

You know what?

The ride's not over.

At least, it better not be over.

Stuart and I are smack in the middle of the top of
the biggest loop of all.

And we're hanging upside down.

# CHAPTER 27

E.

Hang.

Silently.

I feel my body strain against the seat belt and the safety bar. How easy it would be to slip and fall to my death!

Stu doesn't say a word. All I hear are tiny creaks and squeaks as our clothes pull against the seat belts. Something slips out of my pocket and flutters away.

My prize tickets from the Skee-Ball arcade.

Good-bye, prize.

Well, I don't really need the tickets now that I'll be dead.

Oh, wow. Those crackling sounds I heard? They must have been sparks, just like I thought. Which means—

The coaster shorted out.
And that means—
The ride is over . . . for good.

# CHAPTER 28

AN ALARM STARTS TO RING. MUST BE THE ALARM THAT goes off when the ride breaks.

Then I see them down there. Dave and Cassie. Running. They know they messed up. And look at that. They're just going to leave us here!

Stuart and I scream.

Dave and Cassie keep running.

In the far distance, a black BMW pulls into the parking lot.

It's Hal. Come to pick up Dave and Cassie. And that means—

Oh, no! They're really going to leave us behind!

"I'M GOING TO FALL!" I shriek.

Stuart screams back that I'm not going to fall, the seat belt and the safety bar will hold me. I hang on to the safety bar so hard I'm afraid I might snap the metal bar in half.

"Stu?"

"Yeah?"

"Could this—could the whole snake fall off the tracks?"

"No."

"Why not?" I shriek.

"When the cars are moving, centrifugal force holds you on to the track."

"BUT THE CARS AREN'T MOVING!"

"I know. They've got hooks on the bottom of the cars. The hooks run inside the tracks and hold the cars onto the tracks in case the power fails."

Have I mentioned that sometimes in a crisis Stu gets overly calm? He'll go into a whole science lecture about physics to explain why a truck is about to run you over.

"But you know what?" Stu asks.

My heart stops. "What?"

"I just realized something."

"What? What? What?!"

"These cuffs. Hal got them for Halloween, right? They're probably those trick cuffs they sell at Kazam. You give a quick yank and they come right off." He yanks the cuffs but—

Ow! The cuffs don't—ow!—come loose.

I think Stu's losing his mind. Seriously. I think his brain must have fallen out of his skull from hanging upside down so long. Like what do we really care about these handcuffs at the moment?!

The alarm keeps blaring. Then I see— A cop car. Driving into the park. Lights flashing. I watch the cop car drive all the way to the Serpent. YES! We're saved! We're saved! We're saved! We're—

Hey.

Wait a minute.

Why is the cop walking all around the base of the Serpent? What's the matter with that guy? Now's not the time for a stroll. Now's the time for—

Ohhhh, you know what? He doesn't see us! He doesn't even know we're up here!

I scream so loud it feels like I rip out my vocal cords.

What if the cop looks around for a little while and then leaves?

I've never hung upside down this long. I'm not one of those kids who loves to hang off the monkey bars. Let alone one of those kids who likes to hang upside down in a roller coaster car that's stuck at three hundred feet. I can feel all the blood in my body pool in my head. Feels like my face is going to burst.

"What are you doing?" I yell at Stu.

Stu just took one hand off the safety bar, that's what Stu is doing. He reaches into his pocket. "We need to find something to drop down there, get his attention."

Math whiz, science whiz, genius, am I right? What a great idea!

Except—

"I don't have anything," Stu grumbles. "I gave Cassie my keys."

"I've got something," I say. My feet are pressed tightly together over my head on the floor of the car. I rub them together, trying to slip off one of my sneakers.

"Brilliant!" Stu cries into my face.

That feels good. Right in the middle of everything, that compliment feels good.

I never really got the laces of these high-tops tied tight tonight, which is a good thing, as it turns out. Because I'm able to kick off my left sneaker no prob.

We're going to be saved after all!

As the sneaker falls it bumps me right in the face, and I get a whiff of my feet smell. Whew! Smells like corn chips.

I watch the tiny black dot of the sneaker fall. Fall.

And land, right on the track, the bottom of our big loop.

I try the other sneaker. This sneaker hits the track too, but on the side. It bounces off the tracks and keeps falling. Then I lose it in the shadows.

I don't hear the sneaker land.

And neither does the cop, 'cause he doesn't look up.

It's Stu's turn. He works off a sneaker.

Nope. I don't hear Stu's first sneaker land either.

Which leaves us with only one sneaker.

"Go for it," I yell at Stu as he—

Kicks off his other shoe and—

It fallllllls. . . .

PLEASE!

Nope. Nothing.

Four bombs, no hits. We're dead.

And barefoot, too.

# CHAPTER 29

**H**AVE YOU EVER SEEN THOSE SLABS OF RAW MEAT hanging upside down in the window of a big butcher shop? Now I know how those dead animals feel. Hanging upside down in the darkness, slowly twisting in the cold air . . .

If I do a sort of sit-up and tuck my head in, I can see all those empty cars ahead of us in the chain.

I can't hold this position for long. I let my head drop back down.

Way down below, the cop walks around, looking to see if there's anyone around. You want to hear something sad? We fired our sneakers too soon. 'Cause in a second that cop will be right underneath us. If only we had saved our ammo and kept a sneaker. One shoe could have saved our lives.

But we have nothing left to drop. Except us, of course.

Which is when I remember. My lucky golf ball!

The one that Arnold Palmer lost. "Stu! I've got something else I can throw!"

Hey . . . remember how I thought this was going to be my lucky night? Now, where did I put that ball?

I buttoned it into the pocket of my nightgown, under my jacket, that's where. Nice going, Annie. Like it's really going to be easy to get it out of my pocket when I'm dangling upside down three hundred feet in the air. But—

It's our last chance. And I've got to hurry.

"What?" Stu cries.

"Golf ball!"

I can't say anything more, because I'm even more scared than I was a second ago. Because—

I just took my right hand off the safety bar. Wasn't easy. I know I'm seat-belted and safety-barred. Tell that to my hand.

"Hurry," says Stu.

Here's the zipper on my jacket. Not so easy to work a zipper when you're hanging upside down. And you know what? *Great.* The zipper stuck again.

"HURRY!" Stu yells.

Forget the zipper, Annie! I jam my hand under the jacket and rip off the button on the pocket of my nightgown and yank out the golf ball.

Then I hold my hand down toward the ground, waiting, aiming at the cop way down below. I clutch the ball tightly in my sweaty fist. I don't want it slipping out before I'm ready 'cause—

This is really our last shot. Our last chance to make that cop see us. I hope—I hope I hope—I didn't use up all my good shooting luck back at the Skee-Ball arcade.

I squint hard at that cop's blue cap. I move my hand slightly, aiming about ten yards to the cop's right. Okay, Arnold Palmer. Do your stuff.

Then I let go. . . .

# CHAPTER 30

**W**OW.

You know what?

If someone was watching me, they would think I just made the best shot I ever made in my life. I'm serious.

If I *had* to hit the cop, if that was like my goal? I could never have done it in a bazillion years. But see, I didn't really want to hit the cop, I only wanted to get the ball close to him. So instead I hit him smack on the head.

He staggers around for a few minutes, clutching his head with both hands. Then he sags to the ground.

He's out cold.

"No!" I scream.

Stu screams, too.

I'd like to tell you that I'm screaming because I just knocked a man out, but really I'm screaming because I just knocked out the one person who could have saved us.

Finally Stu and I stop screaming.

And then I have a thought that's like the first happy thought I've had since the ride started. It's pretty awful hanging like this, but at least it's not going to kill us, right?

After a long while it will be daytime. People will come and find that cop down there and then they'll find us and save us and—

"Annie?"

"Yeah?"

"We have to do something fast," growls Stu.

"WHY?"

"Because we can't hang upside down much longer."

"WHY?"

"Because—hanging upside down—after a while it—"

"WHAT?! WHAT!"

"It kills you."

# CHAPTER 31

**I** THINK FOR A SECOND. THEN I SCREAM, "WHY?"

"It's an old form of torture," Stu explains. "What happens is—" Suddenly he loses his patience and yells, "JUST TRUST ME, IT KILLS YOU!"

"STU! WE'RE GOING TO DIE!"

Not very helpful, I know, but at the moment it feels like the only thing I can contribute.

"Shut up!" Stu yells back. "Let me think."

Think? What's to think about? How many people will come to our funeral?

"Okay," Stu says, "listen!"

I'm all ears.

"I've got a plan." His voice shakes, but he's back to speaking, not screaming. "We might die," Stu says, "but I think it's . . . our only chance. You willing to give it a try?"

"Why not?" I force out. At this point I'm willing to try anything.

"First . . . we gotta unsnap the seat belts."

On second thought, I'm not willing to try anything at all.

The words from the sign at the loading dock burn through my brain over and over—

WARNING: NEVER REMOVE SEAT BELT OR SAFETY BAR WHILE RIDE IS IN PROGRESS.

WARNING: NEVER REMOVE SEAT BELT OR SAFETY BAR WHILE RIDE IS IN PROGRESS.

WARNING—

"Unsnap our seat belts?" I croak.

"Yeah. Then we'll try to pull ourselves into the next car."

Pull ourselves into the next car?

I try to pull my head up and catch another glimpse of those empty cars ahead of us. My head feels like it weighs about two hundred tons. There's no way I could ever make it into the next car. Not without falling.

"Annie? You with me? We'll pull ourselves into the next car and—"

"WHY?" I scream.

When Stu answers me, his voice shakes even more, but he talks softly. Like I didn't just scream right into his nostril.

"Annie, we're in the middle car for balance, remember? Maybe if we get to the car ahead of us—"

"WE CAN'T!!"

"Wait! Just wait! If we can get to the next car, it might—I'm not guaranteeing this, but it might get the snake started. I think we just need a little push to send the whole chain down the loop."

"You mean—the roller coaster can run without power?"

"No. But gravity will take us down to the bottom of the loop. Then, once we're right side up again, we can climb out and walk down the tracks."

Well, he's right. It's a plan. I don't have a better

one. I don't have any plan at all. Somebody come
save me, that's my plan. And the blood pounds in my
face so hard it makes my eyes squinch up. I can
barely see.

"Okay," I say.

"Okay," Stu repeats. "But before we start, I gotta
ask you Big Favor Number Two."

Whatever it is, I'll do it, believe me.

"Don't fall," Stu says.

## CHAPTER 32

"**I**F IT WASN'T FOR THE CUFFS, I COULD DO THIS WITHOUT you," Stu explains.

He sounds like he feels guilty.

"I know," I tell him.

I believe him. If it wasn't for the cuffs, he would risk his own life and try not to risk mine. That's a pretty good feeling. Except when you're way up in the sky and about to die, it's hard to feel too terrific about anything.

I hear a click as Stu unsnaps his seat belt. I brace myself. I'm ready for him to fly down to his death. But the safety bar holds him.

"Now you."

I hate to say this, but as scared as I was when Stu undid his seat belt, I'm twice as scared when I undo mine.

*Click.*

I feel my thighs strain harder against the safety bar. But I don't fall.

"Okay. Don't move. I'll go first."

If you're waiting for me to say, "No, me first," you can forget it. I don't have it in me.

"Here goes." Stuart swings his upper body back and forth, trying to get up some momentum so he can reach in and get a grip on the safety bar in the next car. He can't reach. With each swing of his body, he pulls harder on my left arm, the one with the handcuffs. Feels like he's going to pull my arm out of the socket, OR PULL ME OUT OF THE CAR!

But then—

He's got it. He's got one hand on the bar in the next car! Which means, he's half in and half out of our car and—

The safety bar in our car flips open!

We both fall!

# CHAPTER 33

S NAP!
I scream.
Stu screams.
Am I falling?
No—
I'm dangling.
I didn't fall all the way!
I'm dangling in midair.
Stu has a hold of my wrist. Stu's holding me up!
That means, Stu must be holding on to the safety bar of the next car with only one hand!
Down below me I see the track at the bottom of the loop. And way down below that—
When I fall, I'm going to bounce off that track just like my sneaker did! Then I'll vanish silently into the shadows!
My weight pulls on Stu's right arm, pulling him down. How long can he—

Wait a minute! Good news! He doesn't have to hold my wrist. We're handcuffed together! But—

Then I realize what—

That snapping sound was. That *snap*! that I heard when we fell—

You know what? Stu was right. These *are* trick cuffs! Because when we fell we snapped them off Stu's wrist. Like magic. Now they're only attached to my wrist.

Which means—

The only thing holding me from death are Stu's five fingers.

And my wrist is starting to slip through Stu's grasp.

# CHAPTER 34

"**A**NNIE!" SCREAMS STUART.

As I slip through his fingers I feel the whole chain of cars start to move.

So Stu's plan would have worked, after all. It would have worked!

But it's too late!

Because as the chain of cars starts to whoosh around the loop-di-loop—

I SCREAM AND—

STU SCREAMS AS I—

Fall!

# CHAPTER 35

FALLING—
Screaming—
End—
Over—
End—
As—
Something—
WHAT?—
Rushes—
Toward—
Me—
Is—
That—
The—
Ground—
Or—

# CHAPTER 36

**1** HIT IT.

I hit the ground.

I'm dead.

Except—

The ground slides forward, back, forward, back.

Then I hear Stuart screaming.

He wants to know if I'm okay.

Am I okay?

I sit up.

I ache all over. I feel like I just broke every bone in my body. But here's the deal. I'm sitting—

Where?

I'm sitting in the front car of the snake. This is so weird. Yes, it's the front car, all right. Look, here's the snake's face, the forked red tongue. And way back in the middle car of the chain, there's Stuart. He's climbing over the cars, coming toward me.

Then I look up.

And it starts to sink in . . . what happened.

The car zoomed around and came down to the bottom of the big loop, just like Stu planned. But how did I end up in . . . ?

When Stu gets to my car, he hugs me and hugs me. I can hardly feel it, like I no longer have a body, but it still feels great. When he stops hugging me, I grab him and hug him back.

Then he stares up at the huge loop of track. "Amazing. That we caught you. 'Cause you were falling straight, so you had a shorter distance to go." He grins at me. "It's lucky this snake chain of cars is so long, see, because the front car got a head start. I'd need a calculator, but I bet if the chain of cars was only twelve cars long, we wouldn't have caught you at all 'cause—"

I don't know what he's talking about. Hello? Is this the time for math puzzles and science lectures, my darling math geek of an older brother? I DON'T THINK SO!

"Come on!" I yell at Stuart. "Let's go!"

We climb out of the car and onto the track. Maybe I did break something after all. I feel broken, but at least I can move. We hold hands the whole way down, like we're still handcuffed. We make it down.

Then we help the policeman to his feet. "Are you okay?" I shout at him.

"Yeah," he mumbles, but he sounds groggy, and Stu and I have to hold him up as—

Two more cop cars arrive.

And before I know it, cops are loading the groggy cop into one squad car and loading me and Stu into another.

"Where are we going?" I ask the cops.

See how my brain works. Never gives me a rest. I'm still worried that the cops will take us to Alston Manor. For trespassing and all.

"You're going home," the cop who's driving tells us.

We're going home.

I sink back into the black leather seat. I feel my whole body relax.

Safe. We're safe. We're safe.

The police radio crackles with static. Now that I know they're not going to arrest us, I'm starting to enjoy being in a police cruiser. Pretty cool in a way. Especially with a pair of handcuffs dangling off my left wrist.

And that's before we pass a black BMW parked out on Stevens Avenue with a cop car parked right next to it.

"Stu," I whisper. "Look!"

There are Dave and Cassie and Hal. The cop's got Hal trying to walk a straight line. He's giving him a drunk driving test! Looks like he got caught for speeding after all, even with his cop uniform. Cassie's crying. Dave's pleading. But from the look on the cop's face it's not going to do them any good. And you know what? I'm very, very happy about that.

I knock on the window and wave happily as we drive by. Cassie and Dave give me a shocked look. Then they disappear into the darkness.

I turn and look at Stu. He's looking at me. We're both too worn-out to smile.

But it's like we're smiling all the same.

# CHAPTER 37

**W**HAT'S THAT?

Did you hear that sound?

Relax, Annie. That was just a branch snapping against the windowpanes of the French doors in my room.

It's after midnight. Everyone's asleep. Mom, Dad, Stu, and Truman, who's snoring downstairs under the piano. I'm the only one who's awake—and shaking.

Five nights have gone by since Stu and I rode the Serpent. I wish I could tell you that I've changed. That now I'm this fearless kid who doesn't need to tag along with anybody.

Sorry. It's still me, Annie Blake, the tag-along goody-goody scaredy-cat extraordinaire. And here's one of the things that really terrifies me. Someone escaped from Alston.

That's right. That thing everyone made so much fun of me for worrying about—it finally happened.

As a matter of fact, it happened the same night that Stu and I escaped from Hilltop. Only they didn't find out the guy was gone till the next morning, 'cause he pulled the same clothes-in-the-bed trick that Stu pulled on Mom.

Anyway, while the convict was breaking out of Alston, I was busy with my own problems. But since then, I've had time to hear endless reports on the TV news. I now quote from the front page of today's *Alston Gazette*—

"Despite one of the biggest manhunts in Maryland history, a manhunt that included a special task force set up by the FBI, the escaped convict, Joe Dodge, has miraculously vanished, a spokesperson for Alston Penitentiary told the *Gazette* today."

The authorities figure this Joe Dodge has probably dodged his way into another country by now. They've gotten tips from people who have spotted him in Florida, Cuba, L.A., you name it.

But me? I still can't help feeling like he's going to sneak right into my house.

I know, I know. Stu keeps explaining to me. When you escape from prison, you try to get as far away as possible.

By the way . . .

I guess I oughta mention.

There is no way to describe how angry Mom is. At us. More at Stu than at me. That's one of the few benefits of being younger. Stu's got a history of getting into trouble. So Mom figures this was all his fault. No matter what I say.

But also, she's plenty extremely furious with me as well.

She says we will never receive an allowance again. We can never go out of the house day or night without permission. We can never watch TV except for the news. And that's just for starters, she says. Dad cut off his business trip three days early so he could come home and yell at us, too, and help Mom think of new punishments.

Stu says we should move into Alston Manor, that the prisoners have it better than we do. But he's pretty scared of how mad Mom and Dad are right now. So he didn't say it to them, the way he usually would. He whispered it to me while we cleaned up the basement—one of the endless extra chores Mom's giving us.

Stu's right. It's like she's sentencing us to a chain gang.

But that's one good thing that changed, I gotta say. Stu lets me be with him now. Okay, he doesn't have much choice, since we're stuck in the house. But it's different. Between us. And he's that way at school, too.

By the way, I wish I could tell you that now that we had this near-death experience, the whole Alston Middle School and High School want to be our close friends. Doesn't seem to be happening. Everyone notices us more, but that's just so they can whisper behind our backs.

Dave hasn't been to school since it happened. Neither has Cassandra. Or Hal. They might get kicked out. The administration is still deciding.

I get the feeling all the kids think it's Stu and my fault somehow, that those guys are in so much trouble. And I can only imagine the way Dave and Hal and Cassandra feel. But Stu says he doesn't care about hanging with those kids anymore, and I believe him.

If only I could be like Stu. Stu feels like he doesn't need those kids anymore. I wish I could feel like I don't have to tag along with Stu so much.

Okay, Annie. Nothing to it. Just tell yourself, no

more tagging. Just say to yourself, you don't need
Stu.

I don't need Stu. I don't need Stu. I don't need—

Wow. The branch practically broke the glass that
time, it snapped into the French doors so hard
and—

I think I'll go wake up Stu and ask him to calm me
down.

What am I talking about? I just decided I'm not
going to tag along with him so much.

Oh, Annie. I have to break myself of these fears
once and for all.

Wait.

I just had the craziest idea. You know how I snuck
out that time? Well, that was with Stuart. That was
tagging along.

What if I went outside the house? Just once. Just
me. Into the night. By myself.

Not outside the complex. Of course not outside the
complex. I mean, are you insane? Never again. But
out into the night by myself. Maybe that would cure
me of my fears.

But what if Mom and Dad catch me?

Hey . . . what else can they do to me?

I tiptoe downstairs. Past Truman. Who makes
those eating sounds, then tucks his head under his
paw. I pat him once. Then take Dad's coat from the
front hall closet. And slip outside.

Down the walk. I throw my head back. Look at the
stars. You know what? This was a good idea. 'Cause
I'm not so scared anymore.

See, Annie. This is the night. This is what you
were afraid of. Nothing to it.

I feel so calm all of a sudden that I start to walk
through Hilltop. I'm remembering how Stu and I
ran and snuck around that night. I stroll all the way
to the Model House. I remember hiding right here.

Right here below the bedroom window where the shade is half pulled down and there are—

Three figures looking down from the bedroom window.

# CHAPTER 38

Okay. Okay, okay, okay. I got scared again, I admit it, but just for a second. Hey, even if I become totally brave and independent, I'm still going to get scared every now and then, right? I mean, that's normal, isn't it?

See, what happened is I forgot about those cutouts. Left over from Halloween. The ones the owners put in the bedroom window of the Model House, just to be cute.

I turn to head home.

And bump into a man with a gun.

# CHAPTER 39

**B**UT IT'S JUST THE HILLTOP SECURITY GUARD. THE SAME guy we snuck past the other night.

"Whoa," says the guard, putting his gun back in his black leather holster. He breathes hard, in and out. "I almost shot you."

Oh wow. Oh wow. Oh—

He glares at me. "What are you doing?"

"Just going for a little walk."

He looks very suspicious. "Tell me what you're up to. Tell me!"

"Ow! Let go! I'm not up to anything. I promise. Just a walk!"

He digs into my arm like it's Dave's raw hamburger and he wants to see my flesh ooze between his fingers.

"—Honest—I just—ow!—I was just going for—a walk!"

Finally, he lets go.

"I thought they told you about this sneaking-out business," he barks. He shakes his head, furious. "Okay, let's go."

"Go? Where?"

"We're going to tell your parents."

I tug on his arm. "No, please. They're sleeping. Can't we just—"

"Just what?!"

The guard marches me back along the path. Now, why did I have to sneak out again? Does anyone remember? If you remember, drop me a line, wouldya? Put it on a postcard.

"Sir? Please. I'm begging you. If you tell on me, they'll kill me. I'm serious. You'll have a twelve-year-old's blood on your conscience, I'm not fooling."

The guard stops, but he doesn't let go of my arm. "Okay," he says, "I'll let you go."

Oh, thank you!

"If."

If?

"If you do me one very big favor."

Here we go again.

Everyone wants big favors, have you noticed that?

"You name it," I say.

"Promise me that you won't ever, ever, ever, ever, ever sneak out of your house again."

That's it? That's the big favor? Boy, am I glad this guard never talked to Stu. He doesn't know how to think up favors.

"You got it."

I run all the way home. And you know what? You want to know how incredibly dumb I am? You want some final proof that I haven't learned my lesson?

I'm locked out again.

But as I stand here feeling cold and miserable, I close my hand around something hard and metal in my pocket.

Feels like—

I pull out my hand.

Weird. It's the keys! That's great, but I sure don't remember putting the keys in my pocket before I—

Wait a sec. It's not my pocket. It's Dad's pocket! I slipped on Dad's coat, remember?

Annie, things are finally starting to go your way. I open the door as quietly as I can. Then I shut it as quietly as I can. Then I hang up Dad's coat as quietly as I can.

I tiptoe up the front steps. I'm about halfway up when I step on a noisy floorboard—

*Creak.*

And I freeze.

But I don't freeze 'cause I made a noise.

I freeze cause I'm thinking, *Three* cutouts? *Three cutouts in the Model House window?*

And just like that, I've got it.

I understand the whole terrifying scheme.

# CHAPTER 40

"**W**HO DID YOU SAY THIS IS? COULD YOU RAISE YOUR voice, I'm having trouble hearing you."

"I can't say who this is, sorry."

I can't, don't you see? 'Cause if I tell the cops what just happened, Mom and Dad will find out that I snuck out of the house all over again and—

"I have to whisper," I tell the police officer. "But the man you're looking for, Joe Dodge, is hiding out in Hilltop Village. In the Model House. That's the first house you come to, right after the guardhouse. Except you gotta be careful, 'cause the guard is in on it. Now please send a car out here—I mean out there. Please! Please!"

"Just calm down, little girl. Calm down. Now first, tell me why you think you've caught the, uh, escaped convict?"

Even though I'm falling to pieces, the police officer

sounds very bored, like he's been answering fake hot-tip calls all night long.

First I make him promise that he won't tell anyone, namely, my parents, where he got his information. Then I make him promise a couple more times. Then I say, "Okay, three nights ago, the night of the breakout—"

"The breakout was five nights ago."

"Whatever. Anyway, that night my brother and I snuck out of our house and—and—and we saw this car drive in here. With its lights off!"

The cop on the phone yawns. "Lights off. Yeah. I'm listening."

I rush on. Telling him everything. Except I keep thinking of new things as I go. The way the guard glanced in back of that car as he checked it in. Now, why would he do that?

'Cause someone was hiding back there, that's why.

*Did you have any trouble?* the guard asked the driver. Why would he ask that? Unless—

The car drives into Hilltop. But not far. Not far at all. Just as far as the Model House.

The house no one ever goes into.

Then we hear footsteps crunch on gravel. Then the car drives right back. That proves someone was hiding in back of the car! Because the driver couldn't have made those footsteps, he was driving.

Stu, you're not the only genius in the house.

Then tonight I see the shade halfway down in the Model House window. Those shades are always up. Plus there are three figures looking out the bedroom window. Three.

But there are only two cutouts. One of those figures was real. One of those figures was—

"Don't you see?" I whisper. "He's hiding out until you call off the search. He's right under your noses. Once you give up looking for him, he can just waltz right out of here."

I'm getting myself so worked up I almost scream. But I hear another yawn from the cop on the phone. I can't believe it. The cop isn't jumping up and down and giving me a medal and putting out an all-points bulletin. He's falling asleep. "We'll send a squad car over to check it out," he promises. "That's the best I can do."

I hang up. It scares me, the cop's voice being gone from my ear. Now I'm all alone. I want to wake up everyone in the house.

"No, Annie," I whisper out loud.

You want to stop being a tag-along? This is where you start. You're going to see this through. Alone.

I climb the stairs. *Creak. Creak.*

I get into bed. And I pull the covers over my head.

I want to wake up Mom, Dad, Stu, and Truman. I want that so bad.

But I wait.

Wait.

Under the quilt, shaking, but silent.

And I wait.

And sure enough, after about twenty minutes I hear sirens.

And more sirens.

And more sirens! Until it sounds like all of Hilltop Village is one big siren and—

Truman, our guard dog, finally starts barking. Mom and Dad's bedroom door slams open. They run downstairs. So does Stu. I take the quilt off my head. Out my French doors I can see lights going on in houses all over the courtyard.

Mom yells at Dad, "Neil, you are not going out of this house!"

But after a while Dad insists on going out to see what's going on. He's gone a long time. Mom makes cocoa for me and Stu in the kitchen. She doesn't say anything. Just slaps the mugs down in front of us, to show us she still hates us. But I gotta figure—cocoa?

This is a good sign. No marshmallows floating on top. But still. Progress.

As soon as she's out of the room, I start to tell Stu what's happening. But I stop myself. It's crazy, I guess. I mean, this is big news, right? I might have just caught the escaped con. I could be a big hero. I mean, never mind what Stu will say. What about Dave and Hal and Cassie and everyone else at school? If I brag, won't they all want to hang out with me, me, me?

Maybe. But right now I'm so into this business of no tagging along that I feel like I shouldn't tell Stu my amazing news. I want to, but I don't want to, you know what I mean?

After about twenty minutes Dad comes back. With this wild story about how the cops just caught the escaped convict, right in Hilltop Village. News that I pretend to be totally surprised and amazed to hear.

"Oh, wow," I say, "really? The security guard was in on the whole thing? That's so scary. Wow!"

Uh-oh. I think I acted a little too surprised by the news, because Stu looks at me very strangely. Like he knows.

And after Mom and Dad finally go back to bed, Stu slips into my room.

"Tell," he whispers.

"Tell what?"

"You know more than you're letting on, now, don't you!"

I giggle.

"Tell me!"

"No," I say.

His jaw drops. "Annie!" He shakes me.

I sit up. Grin. "Okay, I'll tell you." I pause, making him wait. "I'll tell, but it'll cost you a favor."

SUMMER '96... LIVE THE
3-D VIRTUAL ADVENTURE!
T2
TERMINATOR 2
3-D™
UNIVERSAL STUDIOS FLORIDA®
For more information call (407) 363-8000 or visit our web site at http://www.usf.com
© 1991 Carolco Pictures Inc. Terminator 2 is a trademark of Carolco. © 1996 U.S.F. All rights reserved.